# CHANCEY
## *of the Maury River*

# CHANCEY

*of the Maury River*

GIGI AMATEAU

**CANDLEWICK PRESS**

CAMBRIDGE, MASSACHUSETTS

Copyright © 2008 by Gigi Amateau

First edition 2008

Library of Congress Cataloging-in-Publication Data

Amateau, Gigi, date.
Chancey of the Maury River / Gigi Amateau. —1st ed.
p. cm.
Summary: After being abandoned, Chancey, an albino Appaloosa, finds a new home with Claire, who needs him as much as he needs her, but as his blindness encroaches, he and Claire start anew as a therapeutic team.
ISBN 978-0-7636-3439-1
1. Appaloosa horse—Fiction.
[1. Appaloosa horse—Fiction. 2. Horses—Fiction.
3. Albinos and albinism—Fiction. 4. Pets—Therapeutic use—Fiction.
5. Blindness in animals—Fiction. 6. Maury River (Va.)—Fiction.]
I. Title.
PZ10.3.A458Ch 2008
[Fic]—dc22        2007027961

2   4   6   8   10   9   7   5   3   1

Printed in the United States of America

This book was typeset in Horley Old Style.

Candlewick Press
2067 Massachusetts Avenue
Cambridge, Massachusetts 02140

visit us at www.candlewick.com

*For one girl and one horse,*
*Judith and Albert*

# CONTENTS

# CHAPTER ONE

# *Prophecy*

Tonight, the moon was high and full; it cast a light so pure that all fell quiet and still under its watch. Even I felt its pull.

A fire star raced across the winter sky, causing quite a stir among us. The younger ones were afraid and ran to their mothers. I no longer feared the wild streak, as I had in my youth. Instead I dropped my head and gave thanks for a long and good life lived here by the Maury River and in these blue mountains. I gave thanks, too, for the friends who have stood beside me through these many years.

When I was still a colt, I once saw a fire star burning with such a fury that it scared me greatly. I thought it was coming straight for me. I raced to the corner of our field and, unable to find my dam, became filled with an anxiety so invasive that I began to breathe too fast and thus found no breath at all. But I was in no danger. My dam came to me. She wrapped me in her neck, and I was no longer afraid.

My dam explained that when a horse of great beauty or wisdom enters the world, a star chosen especially for that horse lights across the night sky, announcing the new arrival. Dam told me that we should not fear the fire stars; instead we should drop our heads and say a word of thanks for life's many blessings. Dam allowed that occasionally the blaze is so bright and so near that it is frightening, as most things are if you don't understand them. She encouraged me then, and on many such occasions, to seek understanding in all things. I have remembered this for my whole life and only rarely do I feel afraid. When I do, I try to remember Dam's words, then find my breath, and examine that which frightens me.

After that night, I sought out fire stars in the sky. Most nights, I did not see any at all. Sometimes, in the late summer, it seemed that the night held so many that I quickly lost track and would fall asleep watching them, still standing in the field.

"Was there a fire star on the night I was born?" I often asked Dam.

Each time I asked, she would pull me in to her and recount the story of my birth.

"Oh, yes, Chancey. On your night, a star raced across the sky with such brilliance that all present knew you would grow beautiful, wise, and great. Something very special is planned for you."

For years, I believed her; I held tight to Dam's faith that I would become a great horse.

My owner, too, had grand hopes of me. She had planned that I would become a champion, and a beautiful one at that. She bred my dam, a fancy snowflake Appaloosa, to an identical stallion, certain that I would turn out the same, black as night with white snowflakes blanketing my hind. Dam's markings were so vibrant that at her own birth she was given the name Starry Night, not for the sky under which she was born but for the way in which she was adorned with a midnight quilt of icy diamonds.

Yet I am very nearly the inverse of my stunning parents; I was born without pigment. Black stripes do cut through the middle of all four of my hooves, the one physical characteristic I possess which proves to all that I am a true Appaloosa. And so, despite my lack of pigmentation, I believed my dam. I believed greatness awaited me.

Here now, in my old age, I comprehend what I could not before comprehend. I understand now that mothers are apt to wish on stars; every mother prays to heaven on behalf of her child. Sometimes, it seems that a mother's prayers for her child will never be answered at all. Yet is it not possible that one day, when that child is very, very old, he might see that his mother's prayers have been perfectly, beautifully answered all along?

# CHAPTER TWO

*Horse for Sale*

That I had never been sold away was a blessing of immeasurable comfort. I had lived my entire life as a school horse here in this valley. Friends had come and gone, yet my comforts remained constant: the Blue Ridge Mountains, the Allegheny Mountains, and the Maury River all surrounding me. These mountains, all blue to me, were home.

I was grateful, too, that I had lived a life of service under the care of a decent-enough owner. I had seen cruel hands on others, and I was deeply aware of my position. Though throughout much of my life I longed for something more—the greatness, perhaps, that my dam foresaw—I was content to have been treated fairly. My fortune changed, however, when my owner's fortune changed overnight.

The day before had ended the same as most days. We were led to our rooms, given our grain, and the barn was closed up for the evening. But the next morning, no one came to feed us. By the time the sun had moved high into the sky, we all were hungry and panicked. We kicked our doors until finally some of the students arrived to feed us and turn us out.

Monique, the proprietor of the stable and my owner, did not show. That was the first day since my birth that I had not seen her. Though I did not love Monique, I depended on her.

The students who came in her place spoke in hushed tones and whispered of the terrible and sudden death of Monique's husband. These whispers also spoke of a debt incurred by the dead man, a debt so enormous that it might force Monique out of her fine brick home and off of several hundred mountainous acres. In the second it took her husband to release his final breath, Monique had been stripped of her status as a wealthy and privileged landowner. There was no recourse left for Monique but to sell everything, including us horses, so that she could return to her native land, a country so far away that she planned never to return to the blue mountains.

Monique priced all of us reasonably. Many of my fieldmates sold quickly, purchased by current or former students who held a sentimental attachment to their favorite school horses. I recognized these buyers and had taught some of them myself, in their youth and mine. Yet I alone remained—the sole horse for sale.

I suppose, if you have never before been any girl's or boy's favorite horse, no heart longs for you.

With good reason, I was apprehensive that I would be sold at auction in Lynchville. Lynchville held no promising future for a horse like me. In fact, Lynchville offered no future at all, only a guarantee that my remaining days would likely be spent in suffering. Kill sales, like the one in Lynchville, employ unspeakably cruel techniques. Among horses, the code of kill buyers is widely understood—they'll do whatever it takes to load a frightened horse who resists his fate en route to slaughter. I have heard that breaking all four legs or cutting out eyes is commonplace. I would as soon have chosen to fend for myself in the blue mountains and taken my chances against bear and coyote than to have loaded willingly for Lynchville.

Monique warned of the distinct possibility of Lynchville as she appealed to our neighbors to extend some small charity to her by taking me in temporarily. The stables around Rockbridge County had known me since I was a colt. This fact alone should have made it easier for me to find a home, for who would so easily turn away a longtime neighbor now in need? As we set out, I was hopeful that my breeding and years of experience were assets enough to offset my obvious liabilities.

Rockbridge County has never seen a shortage of young, healthy horses. When a horse half my years, and of impeccable health, could easily have been purchased at an attractive price, there seemed no economic benefit to using me as a school horse. Though athleticism and endurance run through my Appaloosa blood, though agility and strength flow into my Appaloosa muscles, though courage and loyalty live deep in my Appaloosa bones, my aches and difficulties defy all this.

My prior career as a school horse had been long and diversified. In my youth, I introduced dozens of girls to the artistry of dressage. I carried many a young man through the mechanics of learning to jump. School horses are rarely asked to jump much higher than three feet, for by the time our pupils grow strong and skilled enough to master an intricate course of twelve three-foot jumps, they are well on their way to competing on finer horses than I. Still, for twenty or so faithful years, I had schooled without complaint, nearly every day and often for many hours.

Monique tried desperately to convince each of the barns we visited that I would make a versatile and valuable addition to their stable, capable of teaching hunt seat, dressage, basic equitation, and jumping. We made the rounds to places I had shown before, all managed by trainers I had seen on and off throughout my life in the blue mountains. I concealed my flaws as best I could. We made no less than four trips to local barns, all of which held plenty of school horses and were not in need of another.

For some time now, my powerful hind had hurt on days when it was too hot or too cold. It hurt me to jump, as a school horse must. This pain was not all that hindered me. My other ailment, I did not like to think about, and for years, had tried to deny. Our neighbors had all heard Monique's complaints about my refusal to jump. They were disinclined, each of them, to believe that I could be of value to their riding schools.

I felt certain that Monique would have accepted any offer made. Yet her pleading on my behalf resulted not in a purchase or even an offer. I feared that the Lynchville auction was my destiny. I resigned myself to never again seeing my blue mountains or feeling the Maury River swirl around my feet or hearing its roar after a heavy rainfall.

# CHAPTER THREE

# Reprieve

L ong after Monique's house, barn, and land had sold to new owners, I remained alone, standing in my field. Though the new owners were horse people themselves, their primary interest was in the breeding of fine Thoroughbreds for the track. They brought no horses with them, as they intended to start a breeding farm only after certain improvements had been made to the buildings and land. As I was not only gelded but also of the wrong breed, not to mention my age, lack of pigmentation, and chronic conditions, the new owners declined Monique's offer of me as a gift. They did, however, agree to let me stay on if Monique would make arrangements for my care until a proper home could be found. I do not know what those arrangements might have entailed as no evidence of them ever presented itself to me.

I had been cared for well enough throughout my life. Like most school horses, I relied on structure and routine. Until this time, I had come to expect fresh hay and a rather healthy scoop of grain twice daily—once to be given just after sunrise and once again in the evening. Now I waited and waited for someone to come with hay, grain, and water, but no one arrived.

By nightfall of my first solitary day, I had eaten all of my grain and much of my hay, and drunk a good bit of water. I remained convinced that the morning sun would bring a caretaker with more rations. Morning came and brought with it a dense fog, but no caretaker. I was not alarmed, but assumed that once the fog lifted, provisions would arrive for me. The fog hung so thick that I could not see even the copper vane atop the barn. For the entire day, the mountains were but shadowy layers of themselves, for there was no sun to light up the trees or disperse the clouds.

I could see nothing of Saddle Mountain, which naturally rises and falls in precisely the shape of an English saddle. I strained to see the highest peak, what would be the saddle's cantle, but it was lost to the sky. Even the lower peak, the pommel, was hostage to the grave clouds which had descended upon me. The unseasonable mix of moist pockets of heat and cold sealed in the fog until nearly nightfall. I finished the hay left in the ring and passed the time by searching for one spot in the field that would give me some glimpse at all of Saddle Mountain. For the entire day, I could not see beyond my own feet.

Long after the fog lifted, I waited there at the gate, sure that Monique herself would show up, or an attendant on her behalf. Only once did I see any activity near the barn. I made a dancing fuss of my displeasure at being kept alone and without suitable food for so long. No one responded to my pleas for help. The activity was not intended for me; workmen had come to survey the barn and surrounding property for the new owners, who had not yet arrived. There was nothing left in the hay ring—nor a fleck of grain in my bucket—and I had resorted to licking the muddy water in the tub at the back of my field. Had I foreseen that I would be standing alone in the back of the field for more than one season, even more than one day, naturally I would have conserved my first day's rations.

During this time of uncertainty, I was consoled by the evidence around me that I was still home. Seeing my blue mountains and just knowing, from the sloping tree line, where I could find the Maury River provided my only solace. Though in my solitude I deeply felt the absence of my former life of comfort and routine, I realized that I remained, after all, in the very field in which I was born.

Upon taking full measure of this fact, that everything I had ever known was as near me as ever, I found it unnecessary to stand a moment longer pacing at the gate, filled with indignation and concern about my future. The new day did, indeed, feel new! With the fog chased off, my thoughts were as clear to me as the blue mountains now on display for as far as I could see in the golden light of morning. I must test my resourcefulness on this land I knew so well, or suffer greatly while waiting for a phantom custodian to arrive.

Fortunately, the winter had been milder than average. I judged by the duration of sunlight during the day that winter had surpassed its halfway point. During Monique's prosperity, the field had held twenty horses comfortably, so I knew I could survive for some time on grass. I also knew that should I awaken to find no grass, I could subsist for a short while on the lichen that covered the protruding boulders in my field. I had seen deer graze in this way, on lichen and moss. With no snowfall, except for a light dusting that had occurred nearer the darkest time of winter, my field was, if not lush, at least sporadically green.

While the absence of a snow cover on the ground

gave me grass to graze, it left me without a ready source of water. Because of my extensive experience as a trail mount, access to the Maury River was as familiar as my own skin. On a trail ride of eight or ten miles, I would often lead riders across the Maury River. At certain points, the Maury runs narrow like a brook—narrow enough that, on a good day, I could jump clear across its banks. At least, in my youth I could. I knew every sycamore tree along its banks and each stark-white river birch, too.

I was even more familiar with the fence line than the river. I knew its vulnerabilities and where it was in need of repair. The front fence line, the side best seen from the road, was made of handsomely maintained white-painted wood. The back fence line consisted of cedar posts strung with barbed wire. A cedar-post fence, if properly constructed, makes smart use of wood planks secured diagonally across the barbed wire between every few vertical cedar posts. The purpose of these diagonal posts is to reinforce the barbed wire, keeping it taut and stable down the line.

Though not ideal for the containment of horses, the barbed-wire fence proved a blessing in my quest for water. I knew exactly where the fence line was weak. I trotted to the place in the fence where the cedar reinforcements had long ago rotted away and used this to my advantage, for I was determined to forge a path to the Maury. It took some work, but I managed to widen a hole enough to give me mostly clear access to the unfenced portion of the farm, which in turn opened the Maury River to me. In pushing open the fence, I sustained numerous cuts and gashes, but none were life-threatening. I grazed on new grass and drank freely from the water. It was in this way that I kept myself fed and hydrated during Monique's absence.

Though I missed the regimen of two good meals served daily, and the warmth of my private room in the barn, I also felt satisfied. I survived, in fact quite well. Near the river, I discovered a lush patch of sarsaparilla, growing just for me it seemed. Though, if truth be told, I prefer the taste of peppermint to sarsaparilla, I found that the pain in my hocks and hips eased considerably when I cabbaged this plant routinely from the forest. A dense thicket of old, proud cedar trees in the middle of my field provided suitable cover, protecting me well from rain and even from wind. And though the winter sunlight cannot be considered harsh, there were times I found that the sun proved too strong for my eyes. The respite of the cedar stand gave me needed relief. I even found warmth there after sunset. I have always been partial to cedar trees, perhaps because of their abundance and familiarity to me. During this time, they proved essential.

As soon as I had secured my basic needs of food, fresh water, and very adequate shelter, my thoughts turned to my owner, Monique. Alone with the blue mountains and the Maury River, I reflected on all that had passed between Monique and myself since my birth. I had known her my entire life. Since I could remember, it was her voice that called me in from the field and her hand that filled my grain box. To my knowledge, I had received acceptable medical treatment, when needed, for both prevention and cure. I had remained active and working. My most basic needs were never neglected. I now pondered as I had never done before the questions of why I had so long remained in her care and why we had grown into such adversaries over the course of my life.

In the many years that had passed between us, horses had been born; horses had been put down for illness or injury. Ponies had been bought for pleasure, then sold for not bringing enough pleasure or not quite measuring up. I knew that I had been spared sale because some part of Monique could never part with her last remaining connection to Starry Night, the stunning snowflake Appaloosa who was my dam.

Monique was so entirely devoted to my dam that she wanted to replicate her in me. Her dejection at my albinism never waned from the moment she discovered me nursing from Dam in the field. She realized right away that she had miscalculated. Not only was my appearance abhorrent, but to Monique and others like her, my albinism was evidence that I was a weaker, flawed specimen.

As constant was her love for Dam, Monique was as uniformly constant in her indifference toward me. Because of Dam's great attachment to me and her sense of purpose in raising me, Monique tolerated me, I believe. After my dam's death, which came sooner than it should have, Monique and I did not replace her with each other, for too much resentment had built up between us. We avoided each other, at best.

As I grazed in solitary confinement, with no horses or people to distract me from my thoughts, I realized I had never before considered the possibility that my dam's death had hardened me, too, as much as it had hardened Monique. Standing alone in my field, the very field where Dam and I were torn apart, I found that what I longed for most was the belonging that I had with Dam and the mares of my field when I was a colt—a belonging that I had not found since. Yet it seemed a prayer that I petitioned too late.

Perhaps I would have been content to stay alone in the field until the new owners completed their work and dispensed with me. Or perhaps I would have gambled all and fled to the blue mountains to start over on my own. The thought of innumerable seasons of fallen leaves whirling under me as I cantered higher and higher up the mountainside was luring me to set out for the forest. Granted, though I had only run through the mountains under saddle, I had always been reliable and resourceful on the trail. The terrain of the blue mountains can be challenging, but I had never lost my footing, even down the narrowest, rockiest cliffs. It would have been a different life to be sure, but I had begun to consider the idea of forging a feral, solitary existence in the blue mountains.

The doorway I had made in the fence line stood open and waiting for me to decide. Though I had spent plenty of time trying desperately to remove my halter, for it cut deeply into my face and I wished it to be off completely, I now began to take heart that the halter had, indeed, been left fastened to me. Halters serve but one purpose—to catch and lead a horse. I had first wondered for what purpose Monique had abandoned me; now I wondered for what purpose she had left me haltered.

One afternoon, as I was again evaluating the option of fleeing to the mountains by way of my hard-earned passage through the barbed wire, Monique herself appeared at the gate and called me to her. I trotted to the gate, demonstrating my eagerness to join with her. Curious, and surprised to see her, I greeted her warmly with a light touch to her chest. I detected a new softness to her, perhaps there all along, perhaps made with grief from the loss of her husband. In days prior, I surely would have objected to my conditions and made known to her my displeasure at the halter having been left so tightly bound to my face. I gave Monique no fight as she hooked the lead rope to my halter. I thought of Dam and her devotion to the woman standing before me and decided that I could start over with Monique, and hoped that Monique could, too.

Monique did not speak to me, so I made the first overture. I nickered long and low into her ear. I blew across her neck with the intent to acknowledge everything we had been through together and also my willingness to begin anew. Monique paused. She sighed deeply and looked around the field, the same field that had once held Dam, the mares, and me when I was a colt. I lifted my head to see more clearly. Was Monique remembering Dam, as was I? The blue mountains encircled the two of us, urging our reconciliation, it seemed to me. I blew on Monique again. I pushed my head into her neck, not hard as if I wanted grain this very instant, but softly, to welcome her home to our field.

I believe now, and will always believe, that for an instant, Monique considered forgiving me as I had just, finally, forgiven her. But the relief that mutual forgiveness brings was not to be. She took me by the halter and pulled my cheek to her face.

"Since when have you nuzzled anybody? Much less me?" She then pushed my head away.

I made no further attempt to reconcile. Monique brushed her hand across her eyes and led me out of the field.

She had arrived with a trailer in tow; I dropped my head and consented to load without a struggle. Unsure whether I was going to Lynchville or someplace I had not considered, I looked toward the blue mountains for what I prayed would not be the last time.

# CHAPTER FOUR

## My New Home

Despite my failure to fulfill her expectations, our lifetime together had entreated Monique to make an act of kindness on my behalf. She had arranged for one last visit to a local barn in an effort to plead my case. The Maury River Stables, owned by Mrs. Isbell Maiden, was the fifth facility we had visited in our mission to find a proper home for me. I knew as we turned into the drive that this place would soon become my home. While Monique approached Mrs. Maiden, I remained in the trailer, watching the two women from the window.

I had always observed Monique to be taller than the averate woman; she had no need of a mounting block.

She always held herself with exceptionally straight posture, which she urged all of her students to emulate. She could not have been credited with exceptional posture on that day. Bent over in defeat and having lost an entire life, Monique made a desperate picture of grief. Wearing dark glasses, and with her head wrapped in a scarf that tied under her chin, she spoke quickly and curtly of the gravity of my situation. The scarf and dark glasses were surely added for dramatic effect, but that is solely one horse's opinion.

Unhesitatingly, Mrs. Maiden agreed to house me, albeit temporarily, with the understanding that Monique would work toward finding a suitable, permanent home elsewhere. I committed myself to expressing only gratitude toward Mrs. Maiden. Even this temporary improvement in my situation, one that allowed me to stay in the blue mountains, was beyond my greatest hope.

Monique didn't seem wholly satisfied with the offer. Rather, she acted quite put upon when Mrs. Maiden suggested that compensation be granted for my food and care, even if only for a portion of it. I overheard Mrs. Maiden tell Monique that she herself had been in the position before of having to rebuild her entire life after a great loss.

"That's why I'm helping you," she impressed upon Monique. "I believe in women helping women."

I maintain that her husband's death and the resulting divestiture of her entire stable and riding school had exhausted Monique entirely of all civility.

"You can drop the women helping women bit," she snarled at Mrs. Maiden. "All of your horses are leftovers like him. Why do you think I brought him here? I've never known you to turn away any horse for any reason."

Upon hearing this, I wondered why we had not started out with the Maury River Stables to begin with, but as we were safely arrived and all seemed to be working out in my favor, I did not make a commotion. I did badly want out of the trailer. Still, I did not kick or snort. I listened to the two women negotiating the terms of my acceptance to the Maury River Stables.

If Mrs. Maiden felt intimidated by Monique, as many people had over the years, she did not show it. Mrs. Maiden reaffirmed her position, "That's true; I love all horses. But I can barely keep the barn running month to month. Anything you could do to offset my costs for keeping Chancey while you get straightened out would help."

Monique acquiesced; she wanted to be done with me. She agreed to send funds when she could, but I believe we all understood that funds would not be forthcoming.

I unloaded agreeably when Mrs. Maiden asked for me. Though I was thankful that Monique's last compassionate act brought me to the Maury River Stables, I had hoped for a warmer good-bye or even some small acknowledgment of our many years together. But my owner had no departing words for me. Mrs. Maiden led me toward the barn as Monique started the truck. I turned back to watch her leave, and stood square as she drove off. Mrs. Maiden waited for Monique's truck to disappear before she inspected me thoroughly.

I gathered that I was sorry-looking when I arrived at the Maury River Stables. I did not request, or expect, the kindness Mrs. Maiden showed me right away by designing a plan to return me to good health. In fact, it was not until Mrs. Maiden's inspection that I was made aware that my health had deteriorated as greatly as it evidently had during my isolated days in Monique's field.

I was first placed in a round pen, where I now understand all new horses are kept for an introductory period of sorts. The day was pleasant enough, though the sun was too bright in my eyes, as I could not escape its glare at all in the round pen. My eyes burned in the full gaze of the sun. By contrast, in my old field I could easily find shelter under my cedar stand, a shadow cast near a hay ring, or even shade thrown off by a tractor to protect my fair eyes and pink skin.

Mrs. Maiden called to a young girl for help. The girl came quickly but kept her eyes cast to the ground as she walked. I judged her to be ten years of age and later was proven correct in that judgment. She was tiny then, and with her dark hair cut short above her ears, looked very much at home in worn overalls and dirty boots. One of her overall flaps was undone and hanging loose from her shoulder. The child didn't seem aware or concerned. I thought I detected a smile when she saw me, but perhaps it was the sun that caused her face to appear brighter.

Mrs. Maiden explained to her, "Claire, this is Chancey. He'll be staying here at the Maury River Stables with us for a while, until he finds a home."

Then Mrs. Maiden instructed me, "Claire is one of my very favorite students, Chancey. I want you to be especially kind to Claire; she's having a bit of a tough time right now."

Claire reached her hand out to me. I nickered at her, hoping she would come closer. She did not come to me, but she did look up to Mrs. Maiden and say simply, "He's b-b-beautiful."

Not one to perpetuate a lie, as I would later learn, Mrs. Maiden said, "Well, he's not beautiful right now. He's a mess. You could make him beautiful, Claire."

Claire did not respond in any way, except to look at Mrs. Maiden and squint her eyes.

Three young girls, obviously just arriving for their riding lesson, strode over to us arm in arm. Claire stepped out of their way. To me they appeared nearly indistinguishable from one another, turned out just exactly as every little barn girl I had ever taught, wearing crisp white shirts, brand-new riding pants, and leather paddock boots. Each of the three wore her hair in a long ponytail. Though I suppose I shall never tire of giggling girls in jodhpurs, I rather preferred the likes of Claire already.

"Hi, Mrs. Maiden," the girls sang in unison. Though the girls looked to be Claire's age, they did not greet Claire, except for the smallest girl, who waved. Claire waved back and smiled.

"Good morning, ladies," Mrs. Maiden boomed. "Go get tacked up quickly. I'll join you in the ring shortly. Stu is up there now with the beginners."

The girls skipped off to the barn with their arms still linked. I continued watching Claire; she showed no interest in joining the trio now preparing to ride.

Claire dropped her head to the ground and quietly said to herself. "Ch-Ch-Chancey's already a gorgeous pony. He d-d-doesn't need me to make him beautiful."

Mrs. Maiden turned her attention from the girls back to Claire. "Oh, but he does, Claire. He does need you. Chancey's been through so much. So much that we could never possibly begin to know, and it's all bottled up inside of him. Look at him. His coat is matted, and

his mane is knotted with burrs thicker than my fist."
Mrs. Maiden tugged on my forelock and lifted my
mane to show Claire its horrendous condition. Then
she pointed to my cheek.

"The poor horse's face is cut so badly it's as if someone slashed him with a knife, though I suspect he
somehow got tangled up in barbed wire. That's exactly
why you should never fence horses in barbed wire—
ever! And look at his legs, all swollen and cut, too.
Claire, when was the last time you saw a horse this thin?
Even with his winter coat, he's nothing but bones. Run
and get a bucket of grain; he can eat while we're cleaning him up," she instructed Claire.

Claire returned in an instant. I waited but long
enough for Claire to step away from the bucket before I
began to consume the grain. How I had missed the taste
and texture of sweet feed! I had not forgotten it, but I
had beaten my palate into disciplined acceptance of
whatever I could forage from the ground. I devoured
the grain with such speed that it must have been shock-
ing for Claire to watch.

"Oh, my gosh. He's so hungry, Mrs. Maiden. I'll
help him," Claire told her. I stopped licking the residue
from the bucket and lifted my head to the girl. She
scratched my ear.

"This horse needs a friend like you, someone he can
really count on. Chancey needs a girl who will love him

for who he is and accept everything he has to offer—then the world will see the horse you see."

Claire stepped closer to me and tentatively reached both arms around my neck. She held me ever so lightly; I felt her eyes close against me.

"Claire," Mrs. Maiden said. "Why don't you ride with the girls today? It's been a while since you've ridden with them."

For barely a second, there was excitement in Claire's voice. "Ride Chancey?"

Mrs. Maiden shook her head. "Not yet. You know he's not ready, don't you?"

Claire nodded, her eyes welling up with tears. Mrs. Maiden squatted down to eye level with the girl. My muscles, the ones with any feeling left, ached deeply. My heart, which had fallen into a very deep sleep over the winter, began to stretch itself awake. I leaned more toward Claire.

Mrs. Maiden put her arms around Claire and pulled her little body in close. Claire wiped her eyes and nose with her hand.

"I want you to listen to me. I know you are hurting right now," Mrs. Maiden said. "Divorce is never easy. I've been there myself and even though it was the right thing, it hurt my two boys badly."

"You have ch-children?" Claire asked.

"Yes, one is grown up now. He lives in Roanoke," Mrs. Maiden explained.

"What about the uh-uh, the other one?" Claire asked.

Mrs. Maiden did not answer right away. Claire did not ask the question again but began picking the mud and rocks out of my feet. Over the years, I have observed that most little girls protest vehemently about cleaning a horse's feet when they are as unsightly as mine were on that day. Claire did the task as if it were only casual work to busy the hands. Not once did she say an unkind word. She had finished with my feet and brushed my entire right side before Mrs. Maiden answered her question.

"My younger boy died when he was thirteen."

Claire placed her hand on Mrs. Maiden's shoulder. "Oh, that's sad," she said.

"Yes, I will always be sad," Mrs. Maiden replied. Then Mrs. Maiden perked up. "You see Daisy over there?"

Claire nodded.

"Daisy was my son's first horse. Boy, were those two a pair; they were inseparable. Here's what I'm trying to tell you, Claire. There comes a day when you have to let go of the pain and let love come back to you. That might just be why Chancey came here, to bring love back to you." She kissed the girl on top of her head and turned back to the business of restoring me.

"Claire, bring me a fly mask from the tack room," Mrs. Maiden said.

"Why?" the girl asked. "The f-flies aren't, aren't out yet."

Mrs. Maiden motioned for Claire to come nearer. "Come here; I'll show you why."

Claire, eager to know why I ought to have to wear a fly mask in March, ran to Mrs. Maiden's side.

"Look at Chancey's eyes," Mrs. Maiden instructed. "What color are they?"

"B-blue," answered Claire, not yet making the connection.

"Yes, they're blue. They're blue, just exactly like yours are blue." It gave me immediate pleasure to know that the girl and I shared something already. Mrs. Maiden continued the lesson. "Now, look at the skin on Chancey's muzzle. What color is it?"

"P-pink!" Claire was enjoying this lesson very much, I could tell.

"Yes, his skin is pink. And his coat is all white, isn't it? These things tell us something about Chancey; he's an albino, or a partial albino, anyway. You'll hear some people say there is no such thing as a true albino horse. Others will say Chancey can't be albino because his eyes are blue, not pink. But none of that matters to us. His eyes are blue, his skin is pink, and that tells us that the sun is harder on him than all of the other horses we know. A fly mask will keep the sun from damaging his eyes any further."

"D-does he have to wear the f-fly mask all the time?" Claire wanted to know.

"While he's with us he will, even on cloudy days, except at night. Run into the tack room now and find him one." Mrs. Maiden dispatched Claire, again, to the tack room. Claire ran off and came straight back with a dusty fly mask, torn at the clasp. She rose to the tip of her toes to adjust the fly mask over my poll. My eyes relaxed. I felt Claire's two hands fasten the fly mask under my neck. She leaned her face into my shoulder and inhaled.

"He smells good," Claire said, while Mrs. Maiden examined me for more cuts and scrapes.

"He smells like a horse, Claire."

Mrs. Maiden didn't look up from behind me. I still felt embarrassed by the condition of my feet, all four cracked and overgrown. Only one shoe remained intact, as I had thrown the others in my effort to widen the hole in Monique's fence.

"I love how horses smell," Claire told her with such pride that I forgot my distress at Mrs. Maiden spending so much time examining every part of me. Claire breathed me in again. Unable to help myself, I inhaled Claire's hair, too. She smelled like a girl.

Mrs. Maiden laughed. "He likes you! Now, grab the currycomb and see if you can get some of this caked mud off of Chancey's other side. Don't rub his face; it's chafed from wearing his halter too tight. And be careful of his legs; they're covered in cuts. We'll tend to his wounds after we clean him up."

I doubted if my great Appaloosa ancestors would have ever wanted to be pampered in this way, but I decided that I quite liked it. Claire did as Mrs. Maiden asked of her, brushing all of me that she could reach and paying special attention to go around my wounds.

"I can't reach all of him. I'm too short," Claire said matter-of-factly, but without complaint.

"Well, then go get a mounting block so you can reach his withers." That was my first indication that Mrs. Maiden doesn't believe in the word *can't*.

The two of them spent an entire morning and most of the afternoon cleaning and bathing me. They soaked my legs in a salt bath of warm water; the moist heat of the water-and-salt combination soothed me. I believe I dozed off with two of my four legs knee-deep in buckets.

Daisy and some of the other mares checked on my progress throughout the day, but no one introduced themselves. I followed the barn protocol set by the mares and stood silently in the round pen enjoying every treatment given me by Mrs. Maiden and Claire.

After the leg soak and a good warm bath, Claire rubbed me down with a towel. The little girl was so serious and devoted to the work of caring for me that I dared not flinch or kick, though her small hands quite tickled. I did flick her with my tail, thinking perhaps she might respond, as flies often do, by at least moving from one place to another. Claire, being a little girl, not a fly, did not move and seemed to delight in the feeling of my tail snapping against her, so I continued.

# CHAPTER FIVE

*My True Companion*

From the first day of my arrival at the Maury River Stables, Claire came to care for me every day, forgoing her own riding lessons to nurse me. She changed my bandages, gave me fresh water, and convinced Mrs. Maiden to move me into a spare room in the barn, where I would be out of the sun. Not once had Claire brought out any tack—no saddle, bridle, or girth had come anywhere near me. Most girls her age would have lost interest after a day or so, preferring to return to the company of the other girls. Claire—she committed to stay with me for as long as I needed. She sensed that I needed plenty of time to heal. I sensed that Claire needed time, too.

Since our first meeting, Claire had not spoken of her family conflict nor the sorrow that filled her. Only once, in fact, did Claire speak of her father at all.

"I'm sorry you d-didn't get to meet my d-dad today, Ch-Ch-Chancey. He had to go b-b-back to work for a meeting. You'll meet him soon; I p-promise."

I rumbled my contentment at the manner in which Claire was brushing my back.

"He d-d-d-doesn't like horses as much as Mother and I d-do. I th-think because he's a-, he's a-, he's afraid. I d-don't, I d-don't see him that much anymore."

Whenever Claire tripped in her words, it seemed to help if she breathed more deeply and slowed down not her mouth, but her mind. I was glad when she leaned onto me and sighed out a long sigh. I sighed out a long sigh, too. I rumbled again. Claire set the brush down, and we leaned and sighed until Claire was breathing evenly.

Had Claire's wound been open to the bone, as was the one she was so gently tending on my leg, I don't know that it could have been any deeper. Yet Claire's wound could not be seen. I was moved to befriend Claire for as long as she needed.

We stood together in my room through the early days of spring, watching as the redbud and dogwood, barren among the cedar and pine all winter, once again bloomed, reminding us both why we loved the blue mountains so in springtime. During our time together, while Claire gazed out of my window and into the blue mountains, I began to think of my dam.

Having lost her so early in life had impacted me severely. Not only did my heart suffer, but I lost my protector. Dam admired my lack of pigment, and it hurt her deeply to see Monique reject me. I was gelded hastily to ensure that my albinism could not further dilute the Appaloosa breed. I clung to my dam and at her death, withdrew into myself. Monique could have sold me then, but I believe we were both clinging to Dam, each in our own way.

My reflective afternoons with Claire stirred in me long-dormant memories. I remembered standing close to Dam's barrel, grazing between her feet. She would push her nose under my neck to invite me to try clover or dandelions. In this same way, she steered me from the buttercup patches in our field that grew despite Monique's effort to keep them down.

While Claire applied a healing salve to my cuts and scrapes, I wrapped my neck around her and ever so lightly touched my nose to her chest. She smiled. Then the sadness clouded her face again, and she resumed her care for me.

I repeated this action of reaching out to Claire, each time softly touching her chest with my nose. Every time, it worked. The touching of my nose to her made the smile appear, and I could feel her breath release. I moved closer to her and leaned gently against her shoulder with my neck draped around her neck. She laughed.

Claire leaned backward into me, and we stood together for such a time that I was greatly content never to move. Claire brought her hand to my cheek. "You're a good, good pony." She did not trip in her words.

Claire reached down for the currycomb; I mimicked my dam's action and pushed my nose under Claire's arm, telling her that I preferred to play. Claire laughed. She reached for the hoof pick, and again I dissuaded her, as my dam had once dissuaded me from poisonous plants. Claire laughed again. I observed that when she laughed, her face held that joy only briefly. Always the grief returned, pulling Claire back into its well.

I touched her neck with my head and the joy returned, this time in a smile. I continued with this pattern until I had proven it true that Claire's bereavement could be healed with a regular, steady application of healing touch. I resolved that during our time together, I would apply frequent doses of touch in an effort to repel the sorrow and keep her spirit elastic and soft. I would recall how my dam had nuzzled me and repeat the same with Claire by wrapping my neck around hers and blowing into her nose. Always we stood this way in my room, rain or shine.

Claire preferred, I think, to talk to me of happy things, for then she did not fall in her speech. She told me of her dream of one day becoming a teacher. I nickered my approval, for I could tell that Claire's kindness and enthusiasm would serve her well in that occupation. I wished that I had been given a bit more of both kindness and enthusiasm myself. Claire described for me how she was learning to make music with a violin. She promised to play for me one day. I listened to all she had to say.

As is the case with true companions, Claire did not speak only of herself. Claire was interested in me. She asked me about life at Monique's. She inquired about my dam and wondered how I was feeling about my new home. We continued in this way of grooming and listening, but not working, each afternoon for quite some time.

Most days, Claire's mother drove her out to the barn after school just so Claire and I could spend an hour or two with each other. Claire's mother welcomed me warmly at our first meeting. "Chancey," she asked me, "are you the pony who has stolen my little girl's heart?

"Well, I'm Claire's mother." She kissed me on the soft spot between my ear and poll. She did not give her own name, and as I had only heard her referred to as "Claire's mother" by Mrs. Maiden or "Mother" by Claire herself, I simply considered her to be "Mother," as did Claire.

The two of them quickly made up for all that I had ever longed for in my life. Mrs. Maiden accused them of spoiling me, for Claire and Mother brought me not only carrots and apples but also oatmeal cookies saved from Claire's lunch at school.

"Listen, Claire!" Mrs. Maiden once reprimanded. "You don't need to feed Chancey all the time."

Claire drew her hand down the side of my body. "But Mrs. Maiden, his ribs are st-st-still showing. Ch-Chancey needs to put some weight back on, doesn't he? I'll stop giving him t-treats when he's healthy again. Okay?" Mrs. Maiden retreated and did not again scold Claire for spoiling me. After that, my treats improved in both quantity and quality.

Claire talked Mother into buying me a most satisfying treat called stud biscuits, which aren't really biscuits at all, nor am I a stud. The little balls of molasses, barley, oats, and I believe a bit of corn, too, were pure decadence for a horse who had subsisted on grass and water for entirely too long.

Mother seemed infinitely content to watch Claire

with me. She often brought a book to read or a writing tablet to occupy her time while she waited. Mother always sat some distance away, taking up neither book nor pen, but watching us. I watched Mother, too, keeping one ear always on Claire and the other turned toward Mother. Claire noticed my curiosity and confided in me, "Mother had a bad horse accident last year. She's kind of afraid now, Chancey. Don't worry, though; she'll fall in love with you, too. You'll see."

I had only a moment to wonder if the petition I had uttered in my old field, only a few weeks before, might actually have just been answered.

Claire threw her arms around me. "Oh, Chancey, I love you! I think you have come here just for me, just like Mrs. Maiden said. You're the most beautiful pony I have ever known."

Had words been available to me, I would not have corrected her that by nearly a hand I am, indeed, considered to be a horse, not a pony. The girl's heart pressed full into mine and for just an instant I felt as beautiful as I was bred to be.

Claire's sweet hand touched the raw marks on my cheek that had been cut into my face by my halter. In that instant, I remembered how ragged I had become. I supposed I had long ago earned my reputation for being hard to catch without a halter. In my alone days at Monique's, my halter had been left on me much too tightly. Had it been loosened by just a notch, preferably two or even better by three, I should not have minded its constant presence on my face. After a while, my cheeks had begun to sting, far worse than the sting of a horsefly or bee. When I had tried to break free of the halter by rubbing my face against the cedar posts and low tree branches, I expect the rubbing also contributed to the rough shape of my face.

Again Claire touched the worst of the injuries on my cheek. "How could anyone leave such a beautiful pony all alone?" she asked. Claire kissed my wound. I felt evermore aware of my condition and ashamed of how pitiful I must have appeared to Claire. Not knowing quite what to do in this situation, I pulled my neck out of Claire's hold and turned my back to her. In this second, I realized how many times in my life I had simply turned away when I felt afraid or confused.

I wished that I could be so much more for this girl—more like Dam, even more like my younger self. How could I let Claire become attached to an old, broken gelding like me? I walked to the corner of my room. I thought surely she would know that my action was meant to separate us until I was again ready for companionship. Even the most inexperienced rider knows that a swift about-face is the clearest form of communication available to a horse. Most people would have understood my gesture to mean, "Leave me alone."

I felt obligated to warn Claire of all that she could not yet see. I had often been noticed, but never mistaken for beautiful. Though my pupils studied under me for months, sometimes years, I was never loved as a child's favorite. I had known horses and people, too many to count. Yet I had never saved a life of human nor beast. I had taught many girls and boys, but never did I carry a champion on my back.

In all my days at Monique's as a school horse, I was a reliable worker but had a reputation of being difficult, even mean. Because my physical body looked so unlike the rest of my band and so unlike my mother, and because my albinism determined me a weaker individual, I was considered even worse than merely common.

And so I turned away from Claire now. I was not expelling her from my space nor my heart, but faced with my own feelings of embarrassment, I needed to escape from *me*. I turned away from everything that came with me to the Maury River Stables and from everything it would mean for me to leave the old Chancey behind.

When I turned from Claire, she did the same to me. Claire walked slowly to the opposite side of my room and, wedging herself as far into the corner as she could, said quietly, "Ch-Ch-Chancey, I thought we were f-f-friends."

Characteristically, as I would learn over time, Claire didn't give up or walk away. My ugliness—in both manner and physical state—had not scared off Claire. On the contrary, Claire had challenged me and decided to love me for everything she could see in me.

"Ch-Ch-Chancey." She called my name again. "I'm n-not going anywhere. We're supposed to be together. You're my only real f-friend here."

I did not move. I stood there in my new room, very much wanting to call out to Claire with my heart, yet unable to do so. I felt Claire approaching on my left side; she squeezed between me and the wall, fully certain that I would not harm her. Most people know that this can be a dangerous predicament; I've seen many get pinned this way, both mistakenly and with intent. I did not pin Claire, of course. Instead, I moved off the wall to give her space. Though I was unable, at that time, to recognize how much I needed to depend on someone, Claire recognized it for me.

"Ch-Chancey," she said. "Mrs. Maiden said for me to let love come b-b-b-back; that goes for you too, p-pony." Then Claire embraced me and whispered, "Don't worry. I will n-never leave you."

Age and experience had taught me by then that "never" is a word often wielded, seldom honored, by little girls. While I was, and still am, certain that the day will come when Claire in fact will leave me, her abiding devotion to me thawed me just enough. I reached my head to her chest, pressed her lightly, and closed my eyes. Claire kissed my cheek again, in the same ugly spot that previously had driven me to retreat from my shortcomings and from her. This time I did not turn away; I held my head to her heart and sighed a long sigh. Claire did the same. I decided that perhaps Mrs. Maiden was right: perhaps it was time to let love come back to me.

*CHAPTER SIX*

# The Maury River Band

My days at the Maury River Stables settled into a familiar routine, not altogether unlike the way in which I had lived at Monique's. On the surface, all seemed very much like the school horse's life to which I had become accustomed. My mornings were devoted to eating and learning about my new home. The afternoons were reserved for Claire. And my nighttime hours allowed me time to reflect on each day. Aware that I had been given an extraordinary opportunity to start over late in my life, I was determined to belong, in a way that I had not at Monique's.

At Monique's, I had been unable to overcome my dam's death. That loss grew, over time, into a resentfulness that would not loosen its grip. While Dam was alive, I had lived happily among the mares. The mares knew of Monique's disappointment at my albinism, and they colluded with Dam to shield me from her rejection. As a colt, I felt protected by all of them. Had I remained with the mares, perhaps I would have found my way after all, for the mares loved me. I did not understand how different I really was until after Dam's death, when I was taken from the mares and placed with the band of geldings.

None of the geldings at Monique's were inclined to protect me. They considered my introduction into their field a direct threat and used all available means to make it clear that my place with them was at the bottom. There I remained for my entire life.

I began my new life at the Maury River Stables on the bottom as well. I had no ambition to secure the top spot in my new home; nor did I wish to live as an outcast any longer. I resolved to find my own place as a member of this band of horses.

I observed that the Maury River Stables was a small operation, with only twenty horses, as opposed to the fifty or so at Monique's. I found the facility adequate, providing everything necessary to enjoy a good quality of life. There was one large, simply built barn, which encircled a small indoor riding ring. Six rooms lined each side of the barn; every room, though small, offered a splendid view of the blue mountains. Saddle Mountain could be seen from the window in my room, for which I was grateful. There was also an indoor wash stall, a cross-tie stall for grooming and shodding, and a tack room. Plenty of barn swallows made their home inside the barn, which Monique would never have allowed. I rather liked the presence of swallows and found their acrobatic performances mesmerizing to watch, especially on days when I was forced to remain indoors.

Outdoors, as at Monique's, all the horses were divided into fields by their gender. The social complexities of geldings and mares are too burdensome for most people to manage successfully, and thus we are more easily managed if segregated. Each field had its own hierarchy of order, and the reasoning behind segregating new horses upon their arrival was to slowly allow the others to acclimate to the idea of opening up to include a newcomer. Right away, I learned that because it was small and tight-knit, the Maury River Stables was a tough band to join, especially for an older horse.

Claire, Mother, and Mrs. Maiden had welcomed me with such enthusiasm that it seemed as if they had been expecting my arrival. Among the horses I encountered some resistance, for all newcomers must endure a period of testing before some place is made. As the mare and gelding fields shared a fence, it was easy enough for the mares to pester me, and they all did, save an old Hanoverian by the name of Gwen, who appeared nearer my age than the other mares. A striking blood bay, Gwen possessed the athletic conditioning of a Thoroughbred and the imposing stature of a draft horse. I thought she represented the warmblood breeds quite regally. Though I could tell that her position with the mares was not what it once was, Gwen still maintained a strong presence among them.

The mares did not introduce themselves, but repeatedly commented, within earshot, on my wretched condition. No doubt they knew that I could hear them, and though they never addressed me directly, I understood that their insults were intended to discourage me. "Look at him; you can see his ribs." Daisy curled her lip as if my smell repulsed her, too. "Why is Mrs. Maiden bothering with him anyway? Horses like him never win at hunter shows or horse trials, and who wants an Appaloosa without spots?"

I find that Welsh cobs, like Daisy, especially the flea-bitten ones, are particularly disdainful of my breed.

A petite Arab, whose name I learned was appropriately Princess, chimed right in with Daisy. "Daisy, you give him much too much credit. He's not a horse. He's a pony, and an ugly one at that!"

"What could Claire possibly see in him?" Daisy asked. She threw her head high in the air.

The gentle Hanoverian swiftly came to my defense. Though I suspected, quite accurately I would later discover, that Gwen had lost her high placement in the mare field to Daisy some years ago, she still carried a great deal of influence with all of the mares, including Daisy.

Gwen wasted no time scolding Daisy. "Princess, I would never expect you to understand. But Daisy, I'm surprised at you. Haven't you been paying attention to Mrs. Maiden? Chancey's been brought here for a reason. Could it be that you're a bit jealous because Claire is spending all her time with Chancey and not you? God made a horse for everyone, and mark my words, Chancey and Claire have found each other, and not by accident. Now, both of you go about your business and leave the old App alone."

Gwen's rebuke quieted Daisy and Princess, but not before Daisy got in a good air kick at Gwen's barrel, obviously missing the old mare on purpose. With a soft nicker, I offered my thanks to Gwen and hoped that her intervention in my defense would bring no injury upon her from the mares.

Princess did not let pass the offense that had been directed at her, however. She grabbed Gwen by the neck and bit the Hanoverian with an unbridled wrath;

Gwen did not squeal, as most would have. She tore herself away from Princess and tore a slice of her own neck off in the process. Daisy pushed Princess into the corner of the fence. Princess had minutes earlier been Daisy's sidekick, but she had overstepped by punishing Gwen without Daisy's authorization. Princess pleaded with the Welsh, "Please, Daisy, no."

Daisy's ears lay flat against her head. I could tell, as could Princess I'm sure, that a severe punishment was about to be handed down. Daisy snorted and kicked until Princess walked farther into the corner. Now docile, Princess once more begged Daisy's forgiveness, for she knew what was coming.

"Please, I'm sorry. I didn't mean to step out."

Daisy paid her no mind; she was making a point to all of us who were watching about just who exactly remained in charge of the mare field. The transgression was serious. Either Princess would take her punishment or challenge Daisy for the field.

Daisy lined Princess up against the fence and delivered a series of rapid-fire kicks to the Arab's belly. She did not stop when Princess began squealing. She did not stop when Princess began bleeding and would not have stopped except that Claire ran out into the mare field crying for Daisy to leave Princess alone. Daisy pinned her ears at Princess, showed all of her teeth, and chased Princess away.

I'll not deceive myself by asserting that geldings are any easier to join with than mares, for they are not. The rules have been much the same in whatever pasture I have ever been placed, though, granted, the new situations that I've found myself in have been few. Regardless, all horses know the rules well.

In the gelding field, I assumed my proper position and challenged no one for a higher spot. Mealtimes presented an excellent opportunity for me to establish that I posed no threat to the status quo. At first, I did not approach the hay ring at all, but waited for the others to finish eating, then gleaned what I could. Under normal circumstances, I would have expected to lose weight right away by forgoing hay, but as I had arrived at the Maury River Stables several hundred pounds underweight, the small amount of hay I was denied did not contribute to further weight loss. In fact, I began gaining weight straight away due to the reintroduction of grain to my daily intake. I stayed away from the hay ring for as many days as necessary to establish my deference to all in the field. I was particularly mindful of the homage due to Dante, the black Thoroughbred in charge of my field.

Many benefits are afforded to the top horse. The field is yours, so you have first choice as to where you will stand, graze, and sleep as well as who you will run with. The boss is the first to be fed, can eat as much as he wants, is the first to come into the barn, and so on. I knew I did not have the strength or desire to challenge Dante or even the short, fat Shetland pony, Napoleon, for a higher field placement. Thus I stayed back at feeding time, allowing Dante to have first rights to hay placed in the ring for all of us. After a good period of showing deference and respect in our field, I finally made a friend in Macadoo.

Despite his intimidating size, Mac is the most trusted and beloved of all the horses at the Maury River Stables. Mac is a purebred Belgian draft, a blond sorrel to be exact. Except for a missing piece of his right ear, a slight flaw to be sure, Mac is a near-perfect example of a Belgian. The Belgians are prized for their considerable height and girth. Indicative of his gentle nature, Mac, who weighed close to two thousand pounds, allowed Claire, who weighed all of seventy pounds, to effortlessly navigate him. Claire liked to call Mac her "big boy." At nearly eighteen hands high, Mac more resembled a tractor than a boy.

Mac towered over Dante and could have, if he were of such a mind, brought Dante down with but a series well-placed kicks, such as Daisy had delivered to Princess. Mac is frightfully intimidating and he sounds so as well, before you come to know him. At the canter, the ground quakes beneath his feet. I have observed his approach to cause people and horses to flee, for fear of getting trampled. Once you have been blessed to know and understand Mac's nature, the sound of his joyful hooves galloping toward you more likely impels you to greet him with equal delight. Indeed, Mac is generous in spirit and eager to be of service to all in need. So gentle and calm is Mac that he is the lead horse in Mrs. Maiden's therapeutic riding school. Mac's friendship eased my transition into the Maury River Stables.

I came to enjoy my breakfast in the field each morning alongside Mac. Mac took his grain beside me, and usually by the time we had finished our grain, fresh hay had been set out in the hay ring by either Mrs. Maiden or her barn manager, Stu. My friend Mac saw to it each day to kick out more than enough hay for me.

In fact, Mac's gesture of friendship was the only reason I was able to eat in peace. Without Mac distracting Dante in the field each morning, I might never have been allowed any hay at all. Just by puffing out his chest and pinning back his ears, Mac would signal to Dante that his throne was in jeopardy. The two would race around the field while I, unnoticed, ate hay to my fill. Once I had wandered off to the back of the field, Mac would retreat, and Dante would claim victory over yet another plot to overthrow him. Such generosity typifies the Belgian Macadoo. He eased the hazing I received from the mares and geldings.

Mrs. Maiden and Stu would bring us in each night.

In our rooms, we would not sleep, but remained awake and listening to Dante kick the walls until even he could not stand his own company. I was happy that my room was next to Mac's, though I would have preferred not to be also next to Dante. Thankfully, Dante did not kick our shared wall for very long before I deployed one of my finest strategies to deflect his obnoxious habit. Though being the lowliest member of the Maury River Band did not carry many benefits, I had by that time learned a thing or two from my many years on the bottom at Monique's farm.

At Monique's there had been a malevolent top horse—a chestnut Thoroughbred—who earned all chestnuts the right to be called trouble. He tortured me day and night. I sustained kicks all over my body; he gashed me with his shoes and bit me on the neck. At every opportunity the horse terrorized me. More than once, I found myself cornered by him, unable to do anything but wait for the impact as he landed kick after kick to my barrel, all for the offense of eating from the hay ring before he had finished.

At first, I ran from him anytime I saw him coming. I hid behind trees so he would not see me. Nothing worked; the chestnut boss was determined to put me down and keep me there. I decided to try something different. I began leaving a nice trail of grain along the top rail of the adjoining wall between our rooms every night. Soon, the chestnut stopped attacking me so violently, and he made sure the other geldings didn't hurt me. Predictably this technique worked even better with Dante, and he soon stopped kicking my wall, which made it more comfortable for me at night.

Nighttime at the Maury River Stables was the hardest for me during the remaining cold nights of spring. In the blue mountains, waking to a snow cover as winter gives up to spring is not at all uncommon. Mrs. Maiden kept the barn completely closed during the coldest nights, and though I appreciated the shelter and protection offered me there, I would have preferred to stay outside. In the barn, even my window was barred shut, obstructing my view of the stars resting above Saddle Mountain. Unlike those horses with thin coats, like the Hanoverian Gwen, I thicken right up in the winter and have no need of a blanket. An indoor room is not a necessity for the Appaloosa breed. I enjoy the night very much, and if it weren't for the pain in my haunches, I should prefer staying turned out in my field on all but the very coldest nights. Even then, I would rather my window remain open for me to see the moon, the stars, and my mountains.

# CHAPTER SEVEN

# A Mother's Intercession

Since my arrival, I had hoped that the Maury River Stables would become more than a stopover for me. As my stay extended into the spring, I believed it would unfold that the Maury River Stables would in fact become my new home. Exactly how this would come to pass, I had not imagined. I knew that Mrs. Maiden and Monique had agreed that Mrs. Maiden would serve as the agent of my sale to a new owner, when the time came. I saw no sign of any effort, on Mrs. Maiden's part, to bring prospective buyers to observe me. I assumed that the campaign to find me a new home would begin when I was again in good health and back under saddle.

Almost every day, Claire tended to me, and I could feel all my wounds healing up nicely. Claire reported aloud on my progress during her daily examination. "Chancey," she would confirm, "I can barely see the cuts on your front legs now. And your coat has nearly grown over the chafing on your face." She continued brushing me, as was our usual routine. Though we had not yet worked together in the ring, I felt it would not be too much longer before I was ready.

Claire was ready, too.

On the first warm day of spring, she arrived to greet me wearing brand-new jodhpurs instead of her usual torn overalls. She also brought a brand-new halter and lead rope to my room. I was quite pleased to hear her say that she had picked out these new accessories especially for me. "Purple is going to be your color, Chancey. Purple is the color of kings and queens, you know. You'll be the most beautiful pony at the Maury River Stables," she bragged.

I allowed Claire to slip the halter over my face. She buckled it loosely around my cheek and clipped on the lead rope. Claire remembered to fasten my fly mask over the halter to protect my eyes. I nickered my thanks to her, for it was only while wearing the fly mask that I felt some relief from the burning sensation in my eyes.

With my new halter and lead rope, and a fine companion guiding me, I was paraded all around the Maury

River Stables. Claire permitted me to eat grass and clover wherever I liked and did not seem to be in any hurry. I grazed alongside Claire for much of the afternoon. Everywhere around us, people and animals welcomed the sunshine, knowing from years past that the Maury River would soon be calling us for a swim, with Saddle Mountain beckoning us to its peaks.

Our pastures overflowed with birds and insects who arrived all at once from the mountain forest, busy in preparation for the day when springtime would truly settle in, bringing with it more daylight and encouragement to stay outdoors. The juncos had gone, and in their place bluebirds now hopped around, collecting horsehair from the ground, then flying off home with sturdy nesting material. As is so often the case, the first days of spring teased that they intended to stay. We all knew better but gave in just the same.

The sun had warmed us enough that everyone felt frisky. Daisy and Princess raced each other around the mare field. Gwen took advantage of their playtime to eat her fill at the mares' hay ring. Daisy wised to Gwen eventually and made sure to dash off a few air kicks as she brushed passed the blood bay. Gwen responded as do all of us living at the bottom: she backed away from the hay as Daisy requested.

Claire and I did not enter the mare field or the gelding field, but rather kept outside the fence line, thus giving the mares another opportunity to taunt me. I didn't mind, for I was with Claire. The new halter and lead rope, and undoubtedly my being accompanied, aroused the mares' curiosity but not their scorn, this time.

Led by Daisy, they all clamored to inspect me. "Come see the old App!" called Daisy. "Get a look at Chancey in his new halter!" Then, for the first time since my arrival at the Maury River Stables, Daisy turned directly to me.

"Well, you sure have changed since you've met Claire. If you're going to stick around, we might at least introduce ourselves. I'm Daisy, as you must already know; I'm the most adored and respected mare here. If you have any business with any of my mares, you come to me first. That includes Gwen. Understand?"

I marveled at the change in Daisy's demeanor toward me, no doubt brought on by my new look. I decided that I very much liked my new halter and agreed with Claire that this purple should be my official color. I also decided that having had some experience with bossy mares over the years, I would give Daisy the respect that she had earned as the top mare. I simply replied, "Yes, ma'am. It's nice to meet you." I tossed my head at Gwen, who had come nearer the fence, though she still hung well behind Daisy.

Daisy had not dismissed me yet. "One more thing,

Chancey, just so you're perfectly clear. Claire's one of my girls, so don't do anything foolish."

Before I could respond, Daisy spun around and kicked her back feet out, stirring up a bit of dust but nothing more bothersome. The mare cantered away.

Claire called out to her, "Daisy, how rude! You must have a crush on Chancey!"

I whinnied across the fence after Daisy, playing along with Claire, who bent backward in a fit of laughter. Again, I whinnied after Daisy, for I liked to see Claire laugh.

Claire's presence most definitely shifted the balance of power, and so as we walked the outside perimeter of the mare field, Gwen walked with us on her side of the fence. Though neither of us ventured to openly defy Daisy, it was pleasant to graze with the Hanoverian and exchange a breath or two. Claire teased me even more after that. "Chancey, I think purple really is your color; all the ladies are interested in you today." As Claire and I continued our walk around the paddock, we drew attention not only from horses but from barn mothers, too.

"Claire, I like your new riding pants. I almost didn't recognize you without your overalls," someone called to her.

Claire did not shrink away or fall over her words; she instead stood taller and beamed. "Well, look at Chancey. Isn't he the beautiful one?"

Everyone did notice my new accessories and the purple contrasting against my white coat. "Look at you, Chancey! What a pretty pony you are in purple!" cried a barn mother who had only weeks before pronounced me depressed. In truth, the opinion of only one of the barn mothers, Claire's, mattered at all to me, and she was not among those passing judgment.

Very early one morning, Mother came out to the barn alone. She did not bring her books, nor her writing tablet. When Mrs. Maiden accompanied Mother to my room, I deduced from their conversation that Claire was spending the day in school. The two women began discussing Mother's desire to purchase me as Claire's first horse. I dared not show my excitement for fear that the greatest wish of my heart might evaporate if acknowledged too soon.

Mother sought Mrs. Maiden's opinion on the wisdom of such a purchase. I detected from the conversation that Claire was unaware of this possibility. I fully understood that Mrs. Maiden was duty bound to help Mother consider all it would mean to bring me into her family. Thus, it did not upset me when the two women inspected me in my room without Claire present.

They stood at my head, one on each side of my neck. I could see Mother best, for she stood to my right. Mrs. Maiden kept her hand on my left cheek, never lifting it, and thus assuring me of her location at all times.

Mrs. Maiden lowered her voice and confided her concern to Mother. "I want you to look at his eyes, because what I see looks like something we'll be dealing with for a long time to come. If you do buy him, you need to know that because he's older, and because of his coloring, he comes with more health problems."

Mother didn't speak; she listened to Mrs. Maiden with her head lowered. She then placed her hand on my neck with a manner of sensitivity I had not expected from her.

"Look at this. When I move my hand across his left eye, I get almost no response. I think he's going blind in this eye," Mrs. Maiden told Mother.

Mother kept contact with me through the entire lecture given by Mrs. Maiden. For it was a lecture—one on my current and future needs should I come now under Mother's protection.

Mrs. Maiden spoke truthfully. This was the other aspect of my condition that I had tried to keep hidden, even from myself, for so long. My sight had been slowly vanishing from my left eye for some time and, to a much lesser degree, also my right. I did not know why it was so. Nor did I know what, if anything, could be done to stop further loss, or perhaps restore my eyesight.

This loss of vision impeded my work and even my very movement. Over recent years, I had learned to compensate for the low vision by going slowly or even refusing to go at all if I had no trust that the rider on my back was skilled enough to keep us both out of trouble.

It was never a lack of desire that caused me to refuse. Most of the time, with enough leg and a few light taps with a crop, I would walk or trot on if asked. Jumping was another matter. Depending on how my rider had positioned my head, I often could not see the jump at all until I came right upon it. Rather than risk injury to myself or a young, untrained girl, I refused, or, more accurately, I ducked out. I was relieved that Mrs. Maiden observed and named what was happening to me. The fear of losing my eyesight had now been my companion for many years.

She suggested to Mother, "We'll need to get a vet out here to run some tests. To me, it looks like he has some kind of growth in both eyes. You can see here in his left eye; the growth has moved well onto his cornea. I noticed it the first day that Monique brought him here. That's why he needs to wear a fly mask all the time, especially in the sun. He's so fair; the sun can really damage his skin and his eyes. I don't know what the growth is, but we need to find out. This might be something serious; if so, you'll want to know before you buy him."

Mother was not dissuaded nor did she seem greatly concerned. I didn't detect, in her manner, voice, or words, any inkling that she might reconsider. In fact, once she spoke, all anxiety I may have had about not joining with Claire vanished.

Mother touched Mrs. Maiden's shoulder. "Thank you, Isbell, for taking the time to point this out to me. When you say this might be something serious, might you mean cancer?"

I did not hear Mrs. Maiden's answer, though I felt an unspoken affirmation pass between the two women.

Mother was not deterred. "I know you're right that there are tests—X-rays and such—that I ought to order before I buy Chancey—"

"That's right," interrupted Mrs. Maiden. "There's a reason for those tests. You don't want to buy a horse that's lame or terminally ill, or in any way unsound."

Often, Mother pauses for so long in her speech pattern that others become uncomfortable and speak their own piece before she has finished speaking. Mother seems aware of her awkward cadence, and I have never observed her to rush herself or stop others from talking over her.

Mother waited for Mrs. Maiden to finish and then continued, still speaking slowly and thoughtfully. "Of course, you're right. But you know and I know that Claire and Chancey have found each other because they need each other. You're the one who brought them together! Even if Claire never gets to ride him—if all she does is come here and groom him—that's fine by me.

I mean, Isbell, Claire has all but stopped stuttering—have you noticed that? She still stutters when she's really nervous, but she's so much more confident and relaxed with Chancey. Besides, what will happen to Chancey if we don't buy him?"

"I don't know. I—"

This time, it was Mother who interrupted. "Yes, you do. You and I both know the answer to that question. Here's how I look at it: the worst case is that we buy Chancey and he turns out to have health problems that are impossible to treat and we keep him comfortable until we have to put him down. Is that the worst?"

Mother did not flinch, as I did, at her statement. I have known only one horse who was put down, for a severely broken shoulder. At the time I did not understand that compassion drove that act. I know better now. I understand that a life of extreme, constant pain and forced restriction of movement is no life for a horse. Still, I preferred not to think of being put down.

"Yes, I suppose that's the worst. You have to consider how heartbreaking that would be for Claire," said Mrs. Maiden. But Mother had already considered all that needed consideration.

"Again, Isbell, the way I see it," she repeated, "buying any horse will lead to heartbreak for Claire sooner or later. Whether she loses Chancey to cancer in six months or old age in twenty more years, it will break her heart.

Besides, you've seen Chancey with Claire; he's got a lot of life left in him. Don't you agree?" Mother leaned into me and brushed her face against my neck.

"Smell him," she invited Mrs. Maiden. "He smells so good." Mother breathed in a long inhale.

Mrs. Maiden laughed. "I'm not going to smell him, Eleanor! You're just like Claire! She always smells him. 'Sakes, he smells like a horse!"

Upon hearing Mrs. Maiden call her "Eleanor," I considered whether I ought to refer to Mother this way myself. She was not, after all, my mother and she did have a perfectly suitable name for a woman with equal measure of strength and grace. She leaned into me and kissed me in what was becoming her customary kissing spot, near my poll. She breathed me in again.

"Chancey doesn't smell like just any old horse. He smells like our horse," she said. I dismissed the notion of calling her "Eleanor." "Mother" it would be.

Horses can detect truth easily because truth is conveyed with not only words, but also with body and heart. Though admittedly, I had not a heart connection with Mother, as I'd had with Claire from the very instant of our meeting, I never doubted that Mother could, herself, see that Claire and I were our very best selves together. Though no money or paper had changed hands, without further inspection or deliberation, I joined with Mother and Claire.

# CHAPTER EIGHT

# A Fine First Horse

M rs. Maiden negotiated my permanent transfer. For some amount unknown to me, the right to call me personal property passed from Monique to Mother. While the papers bound me to Mother officially, it was Claire to whom I now belonged. Neither Claire, nor I, needed a piece of paper or monetary exchange to seal our commitment.

Early one morning, Mother came out to the barn and brought me in from the field without Claire being present. For once, I welcomed the chance to spend the morning in the barn. Our pasture had so trapped the moisture rising off the Maury River that the day already felt very much like the sticky days of summer to come. Flies of every sort and size had turned out in grand numbers to celebrate the return of their kind of weather.

In order to best understand my conditions and needs, Mother had arranged for a collection of professionals to assess my health. Mother and Mrs. Maiden accompanied the experts, with Mother taking copious notes during each examination.

My day began with the dentist, who examined my teeth and then gave no more an exact accounting of my age than I could have determined myself. The dentist explained to Mother that my teeth showed greater depth than width, a triangular shape, and spacing in between. He deduced from these findings what I already knew — that my age was reliably between twenty and twenty-five years, give or take.

"I'd estimate he's about twenty-two," the dentist told Mother.

With that assessment, my official age became twenty-two. Finding no trouble with my teeth, other than their having grown a bit too long, the dentist left for his next appointment with a promise to return soon and give me a proper teeth floating.

I next stood for the veterinarian, whose exam took quite a bit longer than the dentist's. I very much liked the manner of the young doctor. He appeared to have a genuine affection for horses and took several minutes to speak to me before beginning his examination. I learned from Mrs. Maiden that his name was Russ, and his family had kept horses for his entire life. I thought to myself that it must have taken an awfully large horse to comfortably carry a man of such girth and height. I suspected that even as a boy he would have been most at home atop a broad draft horse, such as my new friend Mac.

Doctor Russ's first order of business was to measure me from ground to withers. I recall this precisely because by this time into my residence at the Maury River Stables everyone but Mrs. Maiden had grown accustomed to calling me a pony. Doctor Russ measured me twice and spoke my height out loud, for all to hear. "About fifteen hands," he determined, and made a written note on his clipboard. As the line between pony and horse is drawn at fourteen hands two inches, I was happy to hear that all could now definitely put the matter to rest.

Doctor Russ was pleased with my weight and overall health. He patted my neck. "All right, Chancey. Way to hang tough, boy." He turned to Mother. "Everything this guy's been through? Being abandoned with no supply of food or water all through the fall and winter? I think his weight is fine. He's remarkable— extraordinary, really. But that's an Appy for you, right, Chancey?" He patted me again.

I decided that I liked the intelligent Doctor Russ very much. He seemed a good measurer of horses and quite educated in the distinctive biology of the breeds. The doctor encouraged Mother and Mrs. Maiden to continue generous portions of feed, with the addition of electrolytes to encourage me to drink water.

The constant pain in my haunches and stifles was easy enough for Doctor Russ to diagnose. Without much effort at all—just by feeling me and lunging me through my gaits early in the morning—he gave my pain a name: arthritis. He did not seem concerned that this disease presented any imminent danger, but he gave Mother specific instructions as to its proper management. He told her that I was to be stretched and thoroughly warmed up before riding. Doctor Russ also explained to Mrs. Maiden that for pain treatment I would need a daily supplement added to my grain and a stronger medicine on the days when the pain seemed most severe. The matter of my eyes was determined to be somewhat more complicated, and much more serious.

Mrs. Maiden showed Doctor Russ the growths that she had noticed on my first day at the Maury River Stables. He nodded to her as if he had already intended to tackle this problem. I remained quiet and cooperative. The vision in my left eye had decreased to near blindness; I still could detect some movements, but only from changes in light and dark. I could feel the blindness reach also for my right eye, though not nearly to the same degree as had already occurred in my left.

Doctor Russ explained that he preferred to draw tissue samples to determine the nature of the growths. Mother consented for the doctor to take his samples immediately. I did not move. He proceeded to apply a numbing agent in both eyes, so that I would feel nothing when he inserted his needles. Drawing upon my Appaloosa genetics, I calmly accepted the discomfort, for I knew that no one around me wished me any harm. Doctor Russ removed a stick from his bag and then disappeared into my blindness. Though I could not see him or feel the stick, his presence so near my eye did agitate me.

Mother detected that my anxiety was growing. To her credit, she stayed by my side throughout each step of testing. Had she not been aware of my apprehension, from her own intuition, my involuntary and violent expulsion of loose stool provided evidence aplenty. Involuntary expulsion is a natural tendency for horses in a heightened state of worry.

The compassionate Doctor Russ did not linger a moment longer than necessary. He swabbed both of my eyes quickly, placed the samples in a small tube, and then spoke candidly to Mother and Mrs. Maiden.

"I hesitate to diagnose this before the lab results come back. You can see for yourself that Chancey has something growing on both eyes. Those are tumors. They may be benign, or you may be looking at a horse with cancer. I can tell you this: whether it's cancer or not, Chancey's going to need surgery. Even so, one or both of the tumors will return in time," he predicted.

Doctor Russ left the decision to Mother. "How would you like to proceed? Do you want to wait for the lab results or have me go ahead and schedule something with the eye clinic?"

Mother did not seem at all surprised, nor did I detect any increased anxiety from her. She did not stutter, nor did I hear Mother's stomach rumble, as my own had been since the doctor's arrival. She remained standing near me with her hand calmly resting on my neck and hesitated not a moment before answering.

"If the tumors need to come off, then let's do it. Go ahead and schedule the operation," she consented.

I greatly appreciated Mother's aggressive pursuit of treatment on my behalf. I felt that blowing on her was too ordinary, too common an expression of appreciation. I wanted Mother to understand that my gratitude was sincere, so I licked her. I licked her hand because it was closest to my mouth. I tasted no lingering essence of peppermint or stud biscuit even, only skin. Mother startled before collecting herself.

"Oh, Chancey," she said. Her eyes misted. "Sweet boy." She patted my neck.

Doctor Russ then explained that he would arrange for the operation to take place in Albemarle County at the hands of two eye surgeons. Until then, I did not even know that a special eye doctor existed for horses. Doctor Russ explained that Mrs. Maiden and I would need to make a trip over the blue mountains to an eye hospital for horses, where I would be expected to spend two days before coming back to the Maury River Stables. My anxious stool erupted up again, despite my best efforts to remain calm. Mother kissed my poll.

Mrs. Maiden, having known Doctor Russ and used his services exclusively at the Maury River Stables for a number of years, then asked for the doctor's frank opinion. When Mrs. Maiden inquired, he more willingly speculated a prognosis than he had with Mother earlier in my exam. He did not withhold his belief that my eyes showed cancer, explaining that the shape of the tumors and my lack of pigmentation both contributed to that opinion.

"If this is cancer, do you think surgery will take care of it?" Mrs. Maiden asked.

"Ehhh," he exhaled. "Don't ask me that." Mrs. Maiden and Mother kept silent and waited for his response. Finally he answered: "Depends on how far this thing's advanced. Might be nothing to worry about, or could be we'll need to do more than surgery to keep from losing the eyes. Let's keep the fly mask on him— that's for sure."

Mother agreed to do just that and relayed again her intent to offer me the best care within her means. Doctor Russ left plenty more instructions for Mother and Mrs. Maiden. Most important to me, other than my eyes, my arthritis, and still being somewhat under-weight, he pronounced me perfectly fit to serve as Claire's first horse.

"Chancey's got some health challenges, no doubt about that. But if we take good care of him, Chancey'll make a fine first horse," were the wise doctor's exact words. I took satisfaction that he again made a point of calling me a horse, not a pony.

The doctor and the dentist were new acquaintances of mine, and I had liked them both just fine. Now it was time to turn our attention to my badly overgrown and sore feet. I hoped that the farrier would be just as ami-able. Farriers are a transient lot, more transient even than horses. I have heard Mrs. Maiden say that there are as many as forty different farriers working around the blue mountains.

As yet, Claire and I had not begun working together under saddle and certainly we had not started a course of training, as I was recovering from Monique's unin-tentional, but now evident, neglect. One result of my abandonment in the field was that my feet were so badly overgrown that I had none of the balance required to carry out a rigorous training program with Claire. Even in the field, I had begun to use great caution to avoid stumbling.

When my old farrier, John, showed up, he was a very welcome sight, as was his corgi, Katie. She is a pleasant and encouraging assistant who stays near her owner and never frightens me or disrupts John's work. I have observed, on multiple occasions, that people and their animal friends occasionally reflect one another physically and often also in manner. This was true of Katie and John the Farrier, both reddish in complexion and friendly in countenance.

John the Farrier was deeply committed to his trade, and so comfortable was I with his easy rhythm and solid support of my body weight that it was my habit to sneak in brief naps while he attended to my feet. My bowels had relaxed considerably from Doctor Russ's visit, and I settled right down while John got to work. Mother took great interest in the farrier's craft, and as he began, she offered her assistance to hold me.

"Nah, you won't need to hold Chance. He'll try to fall asleep, so just don't let him fall down on me. He's a good boy. If you ask me, he's as good a horse there ever was. I'd trust Chancey more than any horse I know, except for my own, of course." John the Farrier, I knew for certain, rode a Thoroughbred—quarter horse cross, called an appendix, for I had galloped a field or two on the trail with that red mare.

Despite John indicating that it was unnecessary, Mother held me anyway. She cooed at me the entire time, and while I appreciated her attentiveness to my care, I was sorely lacking sleep and had hoped to get some shut-eye while the farrier worked. Being new to the gelding field, Dante was intent on testing me throughout the day and night, and consequently I was exhausted.

On this visit there was only one old shoe for John to remove, for I had seen to remove the other three on my own when constructing my path through the barbed-wire fence to the river. John clipped all four of my feet and filed them down to perfection. Katie was delirious with joy at the size and volume of my hoof clippings and, being quite the little scavenger, made off with a generous helping of them before choosing one to chew while she watched her master complete his job. John gave me only two new front shoes and told Mother that we could add shoes to my back feet later, if needed.

After he finished, John asked Mother if he could turn me out himself. I was delighted to walk a bit with Katie and John. John praised my purple accessories and let me graze the fence line.

"Chancey," John told me before opening the gate to

the gelding field, "you've found a good home here. I think you're going to be real happy."

I nickered good-bye to John and Katie and hoped that by the farrier's next visit he would see for himself evidence of my happiness. For despite the news that a cancer was likely growing inside my eyes, I knew that something even stronger was now growing inside my heart.

# CHAPTER NINE

# Beyond Saddle Mountain

The return to a regular feeding schedule, the added pain supplement, and, I believe, the companionship of my new friends all served greatly to restore my health. Our only remaining worry was the condition of my sight; the doctor's test confirmed the presence of cancer in both my eyes, a cancer directly related to my absence of pigment and prolonged exposure to the sun.

How many days did I stand in my field in the full sun, feeling it well on my withers and loving that feeling? Yet every day the sun and my eyes waged battle with one another. Undoubtedly, I will someday lose this battle, for no being on this earth is stronger than a star. Knowing the cause of my encroaching blindness, I thought I began to feel my cancer stretching its roots deeper into my eyes, and beyond, with every ray of sun that touched me.

Though no one had offered any hope of improved vision in my left eye, all believed that with aggressive treatment, the remaining vision in my right eye could be preserved for some time. We would need to prepare for a lifetime of surgeries to remove any future carcinomas should they return, as Doctor Russ predicted. To have the malignancies removed, I was to be transported away from the Maury River Stables, beyond the blue mountains and into another valley farther away, in Albemarle County, where cases such as mine were handled every day.

It was an act of true compassion when Mother suggested that Mac accompany me to Albemarle. Claire did not want me to be alone. Mother consented to pay the trailer fee and all lodging costs for Mac to board with me at the hospital that was to save what remained of my sight. Mac gladly agreed to travel with me. I could think of no one besides Mac who would give me greater comfort, except of course Claire herself.

Mother withdrew Claire from school on the day I left the blue mountains for my surgery. Claire did not seem afraid for me and of that I was glad. She spent the morning preparing us for our departure. Claire made a big fuss over Mac and me, grooming us both and treating us to more stud biscuits than was customary. Mrs. Maiden and Mother couldn't help but fawn over us, too. Claire readied the trailer by mucking out dung from a previous trip, filling the hay nets with plenty of fresh hay, and stringing the nets side by side in the trailer, should we feel like eating along the way. When the trailer was ready for us, Claire clipped the lead rope to my halter and walked me inside. Mother followed behind with Mac.

Claire had drawn a picture for me, too, which she had secured to the wall of the trailer. The drawing showed the peaks of Saddle Mountain grandly filling the page, with two friends standing in the saddle between the peaks. The friends—a girl and a horse—nuzzled each other face-to-face. Claire pointed out to me the shape of a heart rising between the two. Then she made Mrs. Maiden promise to keep the picture with me in my room at the hospital. Claire nuzzled me. "When you feel scared over there, just look at the picture and remember me and Saddle Mountain. We'll be here when you come home."

Mother had wet eyes; Claire did not, but stood smiling and blowing me kisses until Mrs. Maiden shut the trailer windows, leaving only a sliver of light visible to me.

Though I could only see slight glimpses of her, I

could hear Claire running beside the trailer all the way down the drive. "Bye, Chancey! Bye, Mac! I love you both! Come back soon!" Claire's words did not stumble once.

I whinnied a loud good-bye and hoped she could hear me, too. I'm sure that Claire stood at the end of the drive waving at us until we were long out of sight. I did not have enough time to say a decent farewell to Claire and Saddle Mountain. The narrow road switched over and back onto itself, and soon nothing of Saddle Mountain was visible. I had lived every day of my life standing within sight of it. Even on the days when its peaks hid under a blanket of fog or behind a blinding white snowstorm, Saddle Mountain and I stood together.

As Mrs. Maiden drove farther away from the Maury River Stables, I lost my breath and could not find it. For many miles, I strained to see something familiar out the window slot. My nervous bowels began to rumble. Mac nickered to me, "You're OK, Old App. The mountain will be here when we return, and so will your girl." I found my breath and sniffed Claire's drawing of us; it still smelled of Claire.

The surgery at Albemarle required only an overnight stay. Again my strong Appaloosa breeding aided me in recovering quickly. Of the surgery itself, I remember only that the nurses spoke very kindly to me just before I felt as if my legs had stopped working and I were going to fall down.

Mac's presence soothed me greatly, for when I first woke up from surgery, I could see nothing at all. The Belgian remained attentive, ready to explain the situation to me.

I feared I would never see again. "Mac, everything is completely dark now. Has the surgery failed?"

"No, friend. Your eyes are both heavily bandaged. I heard them say you'll have the right eye; they don't know about the left. But you will see Saddle Mountain and you will see Claire, very soon."

"Mac?" I asked. "Are you an old horse? You look very young indeed, but you seem older than I am at times. Are you old?"

"Not very," Mac replied. "The dentist says I'm eight."

"I think you are older than your teeth, Macadoo. How did that happen? What brought you to the Maury River Stables? Were you abandoned in a field, too?"

"Get some rest, Old App. We'll have plenty of time to talk when you're well."

I did rest. Mac stood watch over me until Mrs. Maiden came to drive us back to the Maury River Stables. With bandages still on both eyes, I finally returned home. Claire greeted us at the gate, just exactly as she had promised she would.

# CHAPTER TEN

## *Under Saddle*

Upon my return, Claire threw herself enthusiastically into leading my recovery and treatment. Her concern for my comfort never waned; Claire remained as attentive to me as she had been from our first meeting. She checked with Mrs. Maiden to be sure that my medicine was administered properly. She took her role as my friend and caretaker very seriously, and as much as anything, I believe this is what eased my suffering. My eyes healed quickly, and soon enough Claire and I were ready to take our first lesson together, and indeed, our first ride, too.

First Claire took extra time to stretch me, just as Mrs. Maiden had shown her. She leaned her small frame into me, lifted a foreleg at the cannon bone, and then ever so slowly stretched it out fully until I took the leg back from her. After completing each of my legs this way, Claire wrapped both her hands firmly around my tail, braced her legs, and pulled with all her strength. I, in turn, pulled my weight forward, until Claire released her hands.

During our first lesson, we did not jump or practice dressage tests. Instead, Claire asked to practice our flat-work bareback. "I'll feel Chancey's rhythm better if I'm riding free, Mrs. Maiden."

Mrs. Maiden obliged, "Excellent, Claire! Riding bareback will strengthen your legs and core, too."

I, too, preferred carrying Claire without a saddle, as it was easier on my back and joints.

In our first lesson, there was no guessing as to what would come next, or what was expected of the other. Claire asked for a working trot and a working trot I gave her, right away. Claire naturally rose to the trot precisely in time with my outside shoulder. She touched down lightly on my back and without the slightest bounce. Together we two moved in delightful tandem. Claire needed no stirrups, no saddle, no whip, or no spurs. Claire needed only to be Claire. I will say that for the entirety of our first ride I thought only of Claire and what she might ask of me next. I found a new energy, a new appreciation, and a new joy in riding with Claire.

I kept my focus on Claire and tried to forget about the cancer in my eyes. Thanks to the skills of my Albemarle surgeons, my cancer had been halted for the time being. I maintained sight in my right eye, giving me a fair line of vision of nearly 180 degrees, as I had learned from Doctor Russ's follow-up examination. I am faithful to the belief that, had my tumors been allowed to grow unchecked, I would have quickly succumbed to complete blindness. Though I could feel that the cancer remained hidden within me, I could also feel that it had been driven away for the present. In any event, our training had to take into consideration the near total darkness in my left eye.

While neither Claire nor I were beginners, we knew we would have to work hard if we were ever to compete together. Most of my career as a school horse had been spent teaching novice riders only the very basic skills. By the time Claire and I joined, she was already an accomplished horsewoman, as she had learned to ride on Daisy. From the time she was five years old, as Mac relayed directly to me, Claire had spent as much time as possible with horses.

For the first time in my twenty-two years, I felt a sense of purpose in training with one student devoted solely and only to me. Mrs. Maiden set for us a goal of showing in the late-summer series of local hunter shows. Though Claire and I were both experienced, Mrs. Maiden insisted that we start out together in the most elementary of classes—Short Stirrup Walk-Trot. With her undeniable talent for persuasive argument, Claire secured an accord with Mrs. Maiden that if we worked on our equitation without complaint, we could also compete in a jumper class over two small fences. With several months available to train, Claire and I were confident that we would be ready by the end of August.

The focus to our training surpassed any lesson that I had given as a school horse. Claire had chosen me as her companion, and together we worked every day. With the new supplement arriving in my morning grain each day, I felt freer of pain than I had for some time. As Claire and I were not jumping too aggressively, I felt certain that I could tolerate well this degree of soreness and aches. Indeed, it would have been more painful to deny, to Claire or myself, the satisfaction of becoming a team.

True, Claire and I were only jumping small eighteen-inch fences and, at most, a course of two outside lines. But it was a joy for me to be with Claire no matter what we were doing. We progressed easily from taking the little jumps at the trot to taking them at the canter.

We quickly found that I needed to be very nearly completely retrained to jump. As a way of compensating for my poor eyesight, I had long refused or ducked out of jumps. As everyone now understood the reasoning, no one—not Mrs. Maiden, Mother, or Claire—seemed the least bit dissuaded from the effort it took to retrain me. My refusal behavior was treated as an entirely natural consequence of my visual impairment; no one accused me of a poor attitude or nasty temperament.

The burden of retraining me fell primarily to Claire, under the guidance of Mrs. Maiden, and with the encouragement of Mother, who no longer kept up a pretense of reading or writing at the barn. In fact, Mother joined us in the ring by taking lessons, using Mac as her teacher. Mac rather enjoyed this phase of Mother's. He is known to adore human females and is rather boastful of the fact that he has never, accidentally or with intent, allowed one to slip out of the saddle, even at times at his own peril. Mother and Mac got on sweetly. Though they did not train together as Claire and I did, they appeared to enjoy each other's company, and Mother grew comfortable enough with Mac to call for the canter herself every now and then.

The presence of Mac and Mother in the ring, along with Daisy and her new student, Ann, helped us prepare better for showing than if we had undertaken our training privately. As is sometimes the case with bossy mares, one must use extreme caution when approaching from behind. In Daisy's case, she is hardwired to kick out behind her at the slightest detection of another horse. This posed no problem for Claire, or me, for Claire had years of experience as Daisy's primary student. She was well informed of Daisy's invisible bubble and the consequences of violating said bubble. Daisy herself gave off plenty of warning by pinning her ears flat back as soon as any horse even approached her. Daisy's presence in the ring with us simulated the very conditions under which Claire and I would be competing, assuming I could be retrained to jump consistently and safely with Claire.

To help me undo my bad jumping habits, Mrs. Maiden constructed several exercises. First, she began placing dollar bills between Claire's calves and my barrel. Claire was then instructed to ride our entire lesson, even over jumps, without losing the bills from under her. This was necessary, explained Mrs. Maiden, because a strong leg is the best aid a rider has to communicate with her partner. Furthermore, Mrs. Maiden told us that in my case, Claire's legs needed to compensate for my poor eyes.

She said, "Claire, blind horses can compete in Grand Prix events, if they're matched with the right person. Chancey's not completely blind yet; there's no reason he can't do anything you ask him to do. You just have to consistently ask him. If you ask with your hands but not your legs, he's going to have to guess what you mean. Sometimes he's going to guess incorrectly. But if everything about you—your eyes, your legs, your hands, your heart—are telling him the same thing, then it's just as if you were talking to him, like I'm talking to you now. So we'll work on your legs first."

Claire picked up the reins and held the dollar bill tightly against my barrel. For a girl her age and size, Claire already possessed a strong leg; the dollar-bill game only added to her strength.

Mrs. Maiden also had Claire count our strides out loud on the approach of every jump. Beginning about six strides out, Claire would count us over the jump. "One, two, one, two, one, two, jump!" This was begun entirely as a finishing technique for Claire, but we all soon realized that hearing her helped me compensate for my shortcomings. In our training, I learned to keep my ears turning always toward Claire's voice, readying myself for her cues.

"Trot, Chancey, trot!" Claire invited me.

For most of my life, it had been fundamentally contrary to my philosophy to respond to voice commands only, except for the command *whoa,* which I had taken quite seriously. I suppose one of the characteristics that had contributed to my reputation as an obstinate horse was that I required much more of my students than the simple voice command to walk, trot, or canter.

I firmly believe that children don't learn well on push-button ponies, or automatic horses, and so I myself had always determined not to be automatic in any way. Children deserve to learn the basics upon which a strong foundation is built, and that cannot be done through voice command alone, in my humble opinion.

But Claire was different. In working with Claire, I did not feel I was giving her lessons, but learning to move with her as if we were a single being.

"Trot, Chancey," she said again. I obliged. I picked up, and held, an easy trot while Claire performed around-the-world by turning herself around and around in the saddle while I circled the entire ring at the trot.

"And, whoa," Claire sang as she directed me toward Mrs. Maiden, who was still standing in the ring.

A barn mother, watching from the fence yelled, "He's gorgeous. He doesn't even look like the same horse; his coat is so shiny. They look beautiful together." Claire and I came to rest with Claire sitting backward in the saddle. Mrs. Maiden got back to the lesson.

"Okay, Claire, enough play. Let's practice the outside line."

We worked hard to correct my bad jumping habits in time for the summer series. Claire's strong legs became most important to our training. Mrs. Maiden worked us both hard, always pushing us each to do our best individually and to do our best as a team. She liked to pull us into the center of the ring for an explanation of the task before she set us loose to attack the jumps.

"Claire," Mrs. Maiden would say, "you've got to hold him up with both legs. He's not Daisy, remember? If you drop him, he's going to want to duck out, but don't let him. Don't get ahead of Chancey, and don't fall behind him. Use your legs to tell him when it's time to jump. It's almost like you're going to lift him up with your legs, then hold him up the whole way over the fence. He'll listen to you once he knows he can trust you. Remember, he can't see out of that left eye. You've got to see for him."

I learned, with Claire, to wait for that moment where together we would defy gravity. We would canter around half of the ring, with Claire counting my strides on the approach. I felt what was coming from the shift in Claire's weight and the tilt of her head. I felt when it was time to fly.

Claire would rise up from her seat with just enough spring. Steady with her entire leg, and with both of us looking far beyond the fence into the mountains, we would hover for an eternal instant. Once over the jump, Claire would always laugh out loud, delighting in the thrill of jumping with me. She held me straight, and cantering away from the first fence, we would soar, again, over the second fence in the line. We touched the ground, rounded the corner, and again and again we flew over the two small fences, each time with less effort and more lift. During those early days of jumping with Claire, I felt that if I had wings, they would be named Claire.

We progressed rapidly together. My desire to be a great first horse for Claire, combined with my stubborn insistence that arthritis and blindness were mere annoyances, meant that sometimes I pushed myself too far.

Once, after an outside line, Claire reached down and patted my neck, just as she usually did after a clear round. "Let's go again, Chance."

I was already tired and breathing heavily. I didn't want to go again. I wanted Claire to take off the saddle and let me graze in my field while she rested on my back. I preferred to watch the sun set while listening to Claire practice her choir songs. Yet for as much refusing as I had done in the past, I could not refuse Claire. She asked for the canter, and I stumbled.

"Claire," Mrs. Maiden warned, "Chancey's worked hard today. Why don't you walk him down to the barn? You can jump again tomorrow."

Claire's confidence was back; she wanted to jump all night.

"Please, Mrs. Maiden? We're just getting the hang of it together, and I haven't ridden like this in such a long time," Claire begged. "Just one more outside line? Then we'll stop."

Just as I had, Mrs. Maiden also had difficulty refusing Claire. She gave in. "Okay, one more line. Take your time and use your aids; Chancey's tired."

Claire asked for the canter again. This time, I threw my weight into her request, getting the correct lead despite feeling sore and exhausted. Claire counted on our approach and gave me equal support with both legs.

I was not the only one who was tired and needing to rest. I felt Claire's legs evenly on my sides, but then on the approach, she looked away and dropped her right leg. She opened the door for me to duck; I thought I was supposed to go out and so I relaxed, sure that Claire had changed her mind about the prudence of taking these last two fences. I did not expect her to come up into jump position, but she rose into her two-point, ready to jump. I tried to stop myself, but it was too late. I ducked out to the right.

Claire, who was already in jump position, fell up

onto my withers and over to my right. As soon as I felt Claire falling, I stooped and slid my neck and shoulders under her to keep her with me. That save would have made Mac proud.

Mrs. Maiden wasted no time in correcting us. "You dropped him! That wasn't Chancey's fault, Claire. What happened? What did you do wrong?" she asked.

Claire knew her mistake right away.

"I looked down at the ground."

"What else? What did you not do?"

"I didn't hold him up with my right leg," Claire confessed.

"Why not?" Mrs. Maiden always pushed her students, especially Claire, to think about their riding and find their own answers.

"I was losing my stirrup on the right, and I was trying to get it back."

Mrs. Maiden was waiting for that exact detail from Claire. Once she knew the cause of Claire's mistake, she set about fixing it.

"Okay, I know you're both tired, but let's end your lesson right. Try the outside line again. This time, no stirrups." Through our combined willpower only, Claire and I cleared the outside line.

For many lessons after that, we jumped without Claire's feet in the stirrups or hands on the reins so that Claire and I could learn to succeed without them. And so it went, with Mrs. Maiden pushing Claire and me to become a solid team. Only once in all of our training did I let Claire off of my back.

Our mistake occurred on the second in a series of two jumps. We approached from the left, and though I knew in my muscles and memory that there must be a second jump following, Mrs. Maiden had paced it differently; I panicked when I failed to hear Claire's counting.

I ducked out again—in the instant before the jump, I grew impatient, old fool that I am, and second-guessed Claire, whom I had come to love and trust more than any person. This time I was unable to scoop her up, and she fell abruptly off of me, brushing my outside foreleg on her way down. I managed to lift my back leg high over her body, and so we avoided what could have been an accident of serious consequence for Claire.

I knew right away that I had lost her and trotted immediately back to her. I dropped my head down and blew into her face. Claire laughed and blew her own breath across my cheek. "I'm okay, Chancey. Don't worry, boy."

Claire picked herself up and together we took the line again; this time Claire guided me perfectly through both jumps. After our lesson ended, Mrs. Maiden lectured us before letting us out of the ring.

"Claire, you're so good for Chancey. And he's so

good for you. You've really grown together over the last few months. I'd like for you two to show in the short stirrup division next week at Tamworth Springs."

Claire squealed and patted my neck. "We'd love to go! We'll be great together; won't we, Chancey?"

"Hold on, Claire," Mrs. Maiden continued. "If you're going to show Chancey, you're going to have to concentrate. He loves you and he listens to you. Sometimes, though, you get too distracted by other things. Chancey is a good horse; he might even be a great horse. But you've got to help him be great. He needs you to count his strides, and he needs you to concentrate."

Mrs. Maiden let her words sink in before asking, "Can you do that?"

Claire did not hesitate. "Yes! We can do it; I promise."

"You're used to Daisy, Claire. Chancey is not Daisy; he is his own horse. Daisy will jump over anything you point her at. That's why beginners ride Daisy. You and Chancey are a team now; you've got to help each other."

I don't think Claire heard a word of Mrs. Maiden's lecture to us; she walked me down to the barn, all the while making preparations for Tamworth Springs. Claire untacked me and rinsed me off with a cool bath, which I welcomed. She rubbed my entire body with a dry towel and walked me around the paddock before turning me out. We had worked so hard that Claire took extra care to stretch me out again after our lesson.

I leaned into Claire's shoulder with each leg she pulled, enjoying the full extension of my muscles. I looked at Claire, so petite, yet so strong and confident. I realized then as Claire held me, unafraid of taking my weight and holding me in balance, how delicate the matter of balance really is.

When we missed the second jump and I let Claire fall, we lost our balance in an instant. Whether I had dropped Claire or Claire had dropped me made no difference. We had recovered and resolved to go forward to our first showing together. I had never felt better; Claire's confidence was soaring. Our sights were set on Tamworth Springs.

* CHAPTER ELEVEN *

## A Fancy Pony

Claire and I spent the eve of our Tamworth Springs debut together turning me into, in Claire's words, a "fancy pony." I am not a fancy pony. Technically, I'm not a pony at all. Claire prepared me for our little show as if it were a rated show at the horse center in Lexington, where horses from all over the country come to compete. I've been to the horse center, and I'm not the least intimated by the fancy horses and stately brick barns.

As much as I looked forward to our daily grooming before lessons, the beautification that is required to turn out well for a show is something else altogether. Show turnout is a routine that I've been through many, many times with many different riders. You don't get to be a twenty-two-year-old school horse without having your mane pulled now and again.

Claire readied me for the show with a demeanor that I had not seen since that first day of our meeting when Claire barely offered me a smile. I could not relate this girl to the same lighthearted girl that Claire had become. I asked myself, could this serious little Miss be the same one who loved to ride me backward in the saddle? Was this somber girl really Claire, who in the middle of a lesson, would often stop to remove the saddle because it felt freer to ride bareback? My Claire was nervous. She did not speak a word out loud, but the racing of her heart told me so.

Claire dragged the mounting block alongside my right shoulder and began pulling my mane to get it short and even for the show. While Claire silently wrapped thin strands of mane around the braiding comb and then yanked off the ends to make for a uniform length all the way down my neck, Mother worked on removing knots and briars from my tail, which had grown so long that it dragged the ground. Claire and Mother pulled briars and mud from my mane and tail with such steady and even rhythm, I felt almost as if I might melt in their hands. Feeling secure in the cross-ties, I even allowed myself to enjoy a light sleep.

Neither of them spoke a word. Mother, standing directly behind me so that I could feel her presence, knew that I would not kick. With no tentativeness about her at all, she had me detangled in a matter of minutes using both a comb and her fingers. Claire still had not spoken a word, and Mother, too, seemed content to work in silence.

I could hear all of my friends eating their dinner. The familiar smell of beloved sweet feed filled the barn. Though I knew grain and fresh hay would be waiting for me when our work was complete, I felt it more important to stand quietly while Claire and Mother finished than to dance around insisting that I have my hay and grain at once. I liked standing between them, feeling both of them attend to me together, and yet lost in their own thoughts. I liked it very much. Never, I thought, had preparing for a show been so enjoyable.

I closed my eyes and bent my head nearer Claire's heart. Despite her steady hands and quietness, her heart still beat furiously.

"Don't worry," I tried to tell her. "Don't worry, Claire. I'll take good care of you tomorrow." Claire remained too deep in her own mind to hear me.

Claire decided not to bathe me that evening before the show because I love to roll after bathing. A clean white horse will not stay clean for long, especially one who loves to roll, as I do.

There are two kinds of rolling. The frightful kind of rolling is because the pain inside you must be let out. Rolling to relieve pain is often symptomatic of a horse who is threatening to colic. But rolling in the field immediately after a bath is perhaps the most joyful kind of rolling for a horse. Extending all four legs to the sky for a good deep stretch, which then causes the earth beneath your weight to crumble into dirt particles of all sizes that massage your entire back in a most exquisite manner, is bliss itself. No other kind of rubbing or scratching can replace this rolling around with the earth.

Had Claire bathed me that night, we likely would have had to repeat the exercise anyway, because I would not have even tried to resist the urge to cover myself in dirt and dung.

Show day started with a hectic pace. Claire and I were both accustomed to taking our time. We had grown used to our routine of Claire riding me bareback a bit in the field before our lesson, dawdling in my room before tacking up, and then Claire deeply stretching my legs before training. On the morning of our first show, Claire and I did not follow our usual routine. Those around us were impatient to get everything loaded, and we had much to do.

Before light—before breakfast even—Claire and Mother arrived to bathe me. A wisp of moon and one star remained lit when Claire walked into the field to catch me. She did not have to walk far in the dark as I was standing near the gate, waiting for her. After a good night of rolling in my field, Claire often jokes that I am no longer a white pony, but a red one. Not to disappoint, I was anything but white when Claire and Mother arrived on show day. I could not help but roll many times during the night.

Claire kissed my cheek and teased, "You can't be Chancey! You look like a pretty palomino. What did you do with my beautiful albino pony?"

I nickered at Claire and danced around the gate, unable to contain my excitement any longer. "Come on, boy." She pulled me out of the field. "Let's get you cleaned up; you're the reddest I've ever seen you."

Before I could even taste one morsel of my morning grain, Mother and Claire had me secured in the cross-ties and had begun bathing me with cold water. It made for a most uncomfortable start to my day. Claire left the bathing primarily to Mother so that she could load our tack into the trailer.

"Oh, great, Chancey rolled in poo. His whole backside is green," Mother pointed out to Claire.

Claire laughed, which annoyed Mother further.

"Claire!" Mother reprimanded. "Poo is not funny on show day. You know as well as I do that a big part of showing is how well you're turned out."

Mother turned back to me. "Let's get you white again, Chance."

She had brought with her a stack of clean towels and a special shampoo which promised to make even the dirtiest white horse glisten. Mother made no effort to help me adjust to the cold water by first starting with my legs, as Claire would have done. Cold water is more tolerable on my feet and legs; I find that if I can just have a moment to relax, I am able to endure the cold all over my body. Mother was in a hurry, however, and was disinclined to baby me.

I could hear Claire and the other girls near the trailer and could smell the hay nets being prepared for our outing. I could hear Claire, but I could not see her. In a flash of panic, I feared going to the show. I whinnied for Claire. Still wet and cold in the cross-ties, I began dancing from side to side. My nervous stomach rumbled. I wanted to stay with Claire and not let her out of my sight. My routine was off; everything seemed different to me. My bath was cold, I had not eaten yet, nor had I been stretched, and I could not see Claire. I whinnied for Claire again.

Mother tried to calm me. "You're okay, boy. Shhh, you're okay."

I did not respond to her in any detectable manner. I could not find it within in myself to touch Mother's shoulder, as I would have liked to do. I averted my face and turned away.

Finally, Mother dried me off and led me back to my room to eat. I inhaled every morsel of grain and did not pay homage to Dante by leaving grain along the wall between us. I was relieved to taste that my pain-ease supplement had not been forgotten.

Claire came and finished pulling my mane and tried to soothe the both of us. "Don't worry, boy. It's just a little b-b-barn show. There's no reason to be nervous. We've both been in bigger shows than this one, just not together. Don't worry. Everything will be f-fine."

Claire's word stumbling had returned. I sighed a deep sigh to encourage the same in Claire. She leaned against me. With Claire beside me, I breathed easier and knew that everything would indeed be fine. After all, I had many years of barn shows to my credit, though truly I had never shown with a partner for whom I felt as much affection and loyalty as I did for Claire. I touched Claire's chest with my muzzle and nickered deep to let her know that I would do my best, too.

She was not thinking of me anymore; Claire was watching Mother talk, rather animatedly, to a man I did not recognize. "That's my dad! My dad's here! I better go over there before he and Mother start f-fighting," she said. Leaving me in my room, Claire ran to her father's side and hugged him with nearly as much squeeze as she usually reserved for me.

"Dad, come meet Chancey." Claire pulled her father by his hand toward my room.

He shuffled his feet, reluctantly following behind Claire. Though of course my loyalty resided with Mother, who had saved the vision in my right eye and given me a stable home with Claire, it did surprise me that my ears, quite on their own, instinctively pinned themselves back at Claire's father. I caught myself before Claire noticed, however, and stretched my neck out toward him in an offering of friendship. He stood a step or two beyond what was necessary to make a connection.

"Come on, Dad," urged Claire. "Let him smell you. That's how horses say hello."

Mother interrupted the two of them. "Claire, your father's afraid of horses. Maybe if you bring Chancey closer to him?"

Her father stiffened. "No, I'm fine. I can see the horse just fine."

Claire resumed brushing me, chattering with her father about the classes we would compete in later and how hard the two of us had been practicing. Her father began to relax, and I was glad to have met him, for despite my allegiance to Mother, my highest faithfulness was to Claire, and the child was beaming in her father's presence.

Mother stood watching them with her arms folded across her heart. She allowed the two of them only another moment before she interrupted. "Claire, come on. Let's get Chancey loaded into the trailer."

"Okay, I'll be right there. I want to show Dad around the barn first," Claire said.

I could see that Mother badly wanted to pull Claire away from her father, but she did not. Mother nodded to Claire and walked back over to me. She hooked my lead rope to my halter and led me to the trailer. I could feel in Mother, the way she so tightly gripped the lead and yanked on my halter, that the morning was difficult for her for reasons unrelated to Claire or me. I stopped, intent that I should have a moment with Mother before loading.

Mother tugged on the lead; I refused to go. She pulled harder on the rope, forgetting momentarily that I weighed more than a thousand pounds. Mother loosened her hold on the rope and turned to face me. I blinked my eyes at her and threw my head up for her to come nearer. She stepped back to my cheek and rested her face against mine.

"It's just not fair that he waltzes in here like a big hero. He doesn't even want Claire to ride. He thinks it's too dangerous. I get tired of fighting with him about it;

anyone can see how happy Claire is out here." Mother's eyes filled up to the lids with water, which then spilled over onto my neck.

I pressed my cheek into Mother's until finally she began to breathe in an equal and deep rhythm.

"You're a good horse, Chancey. You know, you've saved Claire's life in these past few months. She has taken the divorce so hard. Without you, I don't know that there would have been any joy at all in this little girl's life right now. You've seen her through the hardest thing she's ever had to face," Mother told me. "Thank you, Chancey." She patted my neck softly in one of my favorite spots.

Claire came running up to us, and she was a sight to behold, as her freshly pressed show clothes were already disheveled and soiled from the morning's work. Still, Claire was as radiant a girl as I have ever seen. Mother observed this as well. "Claire, you're beautiful! You and Chancey are going to have a fine time today."

Mother put her arms around Claire and pulled her in so close that I could barely hear her whisper, "Have fun today, my sweet girl."

As the sun had not yet fully risen, I concluded that with Claire nearby, perhaps the sun did not need to wake so early today.

# CHAPTER TWELVE

# *She Fell Up, Then Down*

I believed Claire and I were ready for Tamworth Springs. Everyone believed we were ready. We had worked hard throughout the spring and summer, building first our friendship and then our skills. With each other's help, Claire and I had conquered our respective troubles. We were now a team, and Tamworth Springs was to be our debut. All of us certainly expected that Claire and I would compete without incident. Mrs. Maiden had even predicted that we would come back to Maury River Stables with a champion ribbon, although we were only at Tamworth Springs to get our legs under us.

Hunter shows have never been my favorite. I detest the stressful conditions under which one must compete. The number of times that I've been cut off, kicked, or rear-ended because of rude or novice horse-and-rider teams is not worth counting. But then I am not much of a counter anyway. Coaches and spectators alike move in and out of the show ring with great inconsideration and little awareness. There are those who thrive at hunter shows; I am not among them.

Daisy would rather spend a day at a hunter show than most anywhere else. Of course, because of her sacred bubble, Daisy has always been permitted to show with a red ribbon tied around her tail. Tamworth Springs was no different. The ribbon warned that all who dared to enter the space around Daisy's Welsh rear end would receive a swift, hard kick. I, without a red ribbon to excuse me, was expected to behave amid some quite poorly mannered teams.

If truth be told, hunter shows cause my stomach to clinch up almost instantly with a magnificent force. I am competitive, but prefer my competitors to meet me in an open field. Instead of measuring my worth in diagonals, leads, and head positioning, I prefer that we traverse a course designed to test not only our speed and endurance, but our command of varied and challenging terrain. An event where we are measured by our wisdom, sure-footedness, and resolve to go forward to the end, and without injury is my ideal.

That was not the measure of our challenge at Tamworth Springs. Claire and I were to compete in a most basic set of classes: Short Stirrup Walk-Trot, Short Stirrup Over Eighteen-Inch Fences, and Short Stirrup Pleasure. We expected to place well in all three classes. In some secret place in my heart, I hoped we might win.

We succeeded in placing third in Walk-Trot, a fine enough showing for our first class, though surely not as well as we could have done. There were several factors working against our success. As I've already identified, the crowded conditions in the ring presented difficulty. We did not have ample space to relax and find our spot. We just couldn't get settled. Mrs. Maiden felt the judge erred in not dividing the large class into two separate classes, as it would have improved conditions in the show ring for everyone.

Our third place in the Walk-Trot class was likely caused, in part, by a few strides at the trot where Claire rose to the wrong diagonal, though feeling the error herself, she self-corrected right away. Mrs. Maiden also pointed out that Claire's dirty riding clothes had probably cost us points; she requested that next time, Claire keep her show clothes cleaner. Further contributing was what Mrs. Maiden speculated to be the judge's bias against my albinism. Convinced that we should have placed higher, Mrs. Maiden most emphatically complained to us that this judge was known to despise what Mrs. Maiden gently described as "pink skin" in horses.

Daisy competed in the same class with her young rider, Ann, who, though the same age as Claire, was an inexperienced rider, having only started lessons at the Maury River Stables after my own arrival there. As impudent a mare as Daisy is, she is the pony of choice for graceful, but green, riders such as Ann. With a strand of Daisy's tail braided and tied with the red warning ribbon, and Ann Hayden turned out in two pigtails with red ribbons of her own to match, they presented a classically sweet image, even to my old, jaded, half-blind eyes. Daisy knows her job, and she excels under these same conditions that cause extreme digestive turmoil for me. Daisy and Ann placed fourth in Walk-Trot, a fine showing for their first time out.

Claire seemed pleased with our placement, and she happily tucked our third-place ribbon into the headstall of my bridle. Mother had emphasized to Claire, and to me, that our only charge was to have fun, and not to worry about winning. I noted, however, that Mother was beside herself that we had placed at all, so I couldn't help but believe that despite her protestations about having fun, she took pleasure in our achievement.

In our second class, over the little fences, we failed. I confess that although the entire scene remains vividly indexed in my memory and always will, it is still difficult for me to relive exactly what happened. But for my own conscience, I will try to reconstruct the event as best I can.

Before we entered the ring, it was evident that Claire's anxiety from the day before had only increased. "I f-feel sick. M-M-other, I c-can't," Claire said.

Mother rubbed Claire's back but before she could speak, Claire's father interrupted. "Claire, you're stuttering. You're just nervous, sweetheart. Stay focused. Don't psych yourself out."

With the bit in my mouth and Claire perched too high in the show saddle, which sparkled more than either Claire or I, I had no means to assist Claire in finding her breath as I had done in our early days, when Claire would often tumble in her words, or stutter, as her father called it. I tried to sigh a long sigh, but with so much dust in the ring, the result sounded more like a cough.

Mrs. Maiden motioned for us to walk on toward the gate. Claire patted my neck. "Mother?" Claire asked. "Just have fun, right?"

Mother told Claire and me as we entered the ring, "Right, have fun and be safe!" She patted Claire's leg and then my neck.

"Number one-eighty-five, Claire Dunlap, riding Take-A-Chance," the announcer called out as we entered the ring. I've never been addressed by any name other than Chancey. Even my registered documentation, as far as I am aware, reads Chancey. Claire had wanted me to have an official show name; Mother had come up with Take-A-Chance. I felt as proud at that moment, hearing my new show name called along with Claire's, as I ever have in my life.

I know that we took the first jump fine. Six strides out, I saw the jump clearly and straight ahead of us. I heard Claire counting, "One, two, one, two, one, two." I had come rely on her counting to compensate for the darkness in my left eye. Claire's voice command— "Jump!"—accompanied by an even squeeze of her legs and the raising of her hands to be nearer my ears, aided me in flying over the jump, as we had practiced in our training. We attacked the fence with purpose and unison. I listened for Claire's breathing, but could not find it.

Still, our first small fence was textbook. I felt it to be so, and as we passed by, I heard Mrs. Maiden call out to us, "Perfect!"

We completed the first jump and, cantering away, rounded the ring toward the left. I did not relax a bit, for Claire had not. I listened closely for her second wave of counting. I saw Claire's father out of my right eye; I'm certain that Claire saw him, too, for I felt the slightest tilt of her head in his direction. She was so proud that he had come to see her. Claire sat higher in the saddle, making little contact with me.

Perhaps, had the two jumps been placed in a simple line with two strides in between, the day would have ended pleasantly. On the second approach, Claire did not count, and I did not feel her legs firm on me as I had at our first jump. I could not find Claire's aids—neither her legs nor voice instructed me. Nor could my right eye find the second jump, and so I wavered. Not until late in our approach did I see the jump at all.

When the fence did appear, dead-on in front of me, I panicked, unsure what Claire meant for me to do next. She failed to move into jump position. I did not refuse the jump straight on by stopping, for having gathered a nice speed, I knew that an abrupt halt, even if Claire was intending our retreat, would likely throw her over my head. Not feeling Claire's right leg resisting my duck, I did not aim to take the fence—though in looking back, I know I could have managed to barrel through it, had I kept my wits. I swerved out to the right without breaking stride and without Claire. She was so light.

To my right and just behind me, I saw Claire fall, first up and then down. I could do nothing. I heard her helmet crack against the ground. In unison, the spectators gasped for air. I whipped quickly around, but in the slowest measure of time could only watch Claire bounce off of her head and come to a rest near the jump rail.

I galloped back to Claire, slowing to a walk only when I came directly upon her. Reaching her before anyone else, I bowed my head and blew across her face. Her eyes remained closed, and nothing of Claire moved. I blew again, this time closer to her face, and waited to catch the smell of her breath back to me. I could find no breath, no smell of Claire, only a great weight in my chest. I found no voice of my own to call for help. Everyone around us moved about slowly, too slowly. In those first few moments of Claire's unconsciousness, I had no one to help me revive Claire.

Some horses beg and spend their entire lives begging. Whatever they do get is never enough and they beg for more, constantly. I have probably not asked for enough in my life. At Tamworth Springs I asked for Claire. In fact, I begged for Claire. I didn't ponder it. I fell to my knees to be nearer to Claire and simultaneously to beg my Creator, and Claire's, to awaken her quickly with either my breath or His. I lay beside Claire.

As I set my head near Claire's, again I heard the crowd suck in their own collective breath. I could not speak to Claire but with my heart, and with it I showed her everything we had yet to do. There was still Saddle Mountain to be explored. I had yet to take Claire across the Maury River. She had promised to play her violin for me. We had planned to one day gallop through the snow.

I gave my breath to Claire. I begged Claire to wake up and forgive me for dropping her. My prayers for her restoration were interrupted by a change of pace; everyone who had been so slow to reach us now descended upon us. My stomach tightened. I remained on the ground next to Claire.

"Get that horse away from my daughter," Claire's father demanded. I looked to Mother for protection, for she was now kneeling beside us. Mother took no notice of me or the command that I be removed from the show ring.

Instead, Mother began yelling for help. I stood up and with my voice strong now, joined with Mother and whinnied long and shrill to better relay our urgent need for assistance. Still, Claire did not move, nor did she answer the questions that Mrs. Maiden had begun asking to ascertain whether Claire was damaged by the impact of the fall.

Daisy, carrying Ann, stood at the entrance to the show ring, watching our attempts. Daisy tossed her head toward me, but that was of small comfort.

Claire's father spoke sharply under his breath to Mother. "For God's sake, Eleanor, I told you this would happen. What were you thinking? The horse is dangerous; he's half blind."

My chest tightened; a weakness grew there and

spread within me. I felt the brick in my stomach churn. I dropped my head down toward Claire. I wanted to roll.

Mother stayed crouched beside Claire, holding her hand. She did not look up.

Still, Claire's father persisted. "Eleanor? Did you hear me? That's it; it's over. The horse needs to be sold. He's hurt Claire. Do you understand? We're getting rid of him."

Mother said nothing. She held Claire's hand and kissed her forehead again and again.

Claire's father said to no one in particular, "Will someone get this horse out of here? He's hurt my daughter. He needs to be taken away."

Mother did not look up and did not speak. I stood by Mother, for she needed me and so did Claire. I stepped in closer, for I belonged with them.

Claire remained motionless; again I blew a long breath out, across her nose and mouth. My girl opened her eyes, but I gather was not altogether restored.

More people joined us, and the biased judge grabbed my reins to lead me out of the ring. I refused to go and sank all of my one thousand pounds as far into the earth as I could. The judge, with warmth that I did not expect, turned to face me and patted my shoulder. "Come on, fella. The rescue squad will take good care of her."

I whinnied at Claire. She did not respond. I whinnied at Mother. Mother looked up at me with her sad eyes. She smiled at me and finally opened her mouth to speak.

"Please, Eleanor, this horse has got to go!" shouted Claire's father.

He snatched my reins from the judge and began pulling on me. He yanked hard on my mouth, but for Mother and Claire I absorbed the pain because I would not leave them. Mother jumped up and took the reins from his hand. Without shouting, she faced him squarely and told him, "Chancey is our horse. You don't get to decide. He's not your horse."

Mother handed the reins back to the judge. Then she kissed my poll and whispered in my ear, her voice cracking, "You're going home now, Chancey. I'm going with Claire. You belong with us; don't ever forget that, boy."

The judge again tried to comfort me. "That's a boy; come with me. Claire will be just fine." Her voice conveyed no pigment bias toward me whatsoever. I yielded to the judge's pull and watched the rescue squad take Claire and Mother away.

* CHAPTER THIRTEEN *

## *Waiting Out the Storm*

I ached to leave Tamworth Springs at the instant that Claire left, but was required to stay on, as we had all traveled there together for the purpose of allowing Claire and Ann to compete. Mrs. Maiden took my reins from the judge and thanked her for holding me. I could think of nothing but Claire. I did everything to slow my breathing, yet it remained fast and shallow.

The judge resumed her post. After a moment, the announcer started the class again. "Short Stirrup Over Eighteen-Inch Fences. Number one-eighty-six, Ann Hayden, riding Shasta Daisy."

We waited for Daisy and Ann to enter the ring. Ann wouldn't budge, but motioned for Mrs. Maiden. The child was understandably shaken up. She did not try to choke back her tears. "I want to get off now. I don't want to jump," she cried.

Mrs. Maiden spoke gently to her. "Are you sure? Take a deep breath. Trust Daisy; you'll be fine. Can you do that?"

Ann opened her mouth and breathed. She looked at the show ring and patted Daisy's neck. Daisy stood still and quiet; she did not dance or shift her weight at all. She waited for Ann to decide. Mrs. Maiden encouraged the girl to breathe in deep.

Finally, Ann said, "OK. I'm OK." She picked up the reins and clucked for Daisy to walk on.

Daisy did her job. She was, I believe, born for the purpose of taking little girls over little fences. Ann did not count, for on Daisy little girls need only to sit deep, look graceful, and trust. The pair took the two little jumps superbly, placing first in the class.

Though I stood beside Mrs. Maiden watching the event, I could only see the image in my mind of Claire sprawled on the ground and Mother kissing her face to wake her up. There was much noise around me, yet nothing could deafen to me the sound of Claire's father saying, "The horse is dangerous. This horse needs to be sold."

The words of Claire's father and the image of Claire, whom I had hurt, began to tangle themselves together until the pain of the morning had woven itself into severe knots deep inside my gut. Reflexively, I began biting and kicking at my sides in an effort to disperse the knots and free myself from the memories of the morning. I needed to get home.

After the end of the jumper class, I began to dance around with enough fuss that Mrs. Maiden knew to take me back to the trailer. I could not watch the Pleasure class. I wanted to roll, not for the joy of rolling, but to break up what had become the constant cramping in my belly. Right there at Tamworth Springs, I badly wanted to roll and never get up. I did not give in. I waited at the trailer for my teammates' return.

Though it may have appeared that I waited quietly, on the inside I twisted with pain and regret. Every second that passed was more horrific than the one that preceded it, for it brought no relief from the tangles, no relief from the guilt, and no relief from the certain knowledge that my future with Claire was in jeopardy.

When it came time to depart Tamworth Springs, I loaded easily into the trailer as is mostly my habit anyway. Daisy, Ann, Mrs. Maiden, and I drove back to our barn without Claire. In the trailer, Daisy tried to comfort me. "Don't worry. Claire's a tough little girl. I've known her a long time. She'll hold no grudge against you."

I appreciated Daisy's sympathy, and it softened me toward her greatly, as I confess, I still held sourness in my heart concerning the flea-bitten Welsh.

Though I would have preferred that Macadoo, my friend and fieldmate, the Belgian who had traveled with me to Albemarle and who had helped me find my place among the geldings, be the one to see me in this state of vulnerability, I found myself in such desperate need of assurance that I willingly risked reaching out to Daisy.

"Daisy? What if the girl's father is right? He said I am dangerous. He said I need to be sold." I rumbled softly, feeling some relief at letting another know what had occurred in the show ring. I hoped I was not foolish to seek some affirmation from the mare.

Daisy moved closer to me. She offered no comforting exchange of breaths. Nor did we touch noses.

"You know you'll never be a jumper of the caliber that I am. That's a fact you have to face. The sooner you do face it, the better for you and for Claire. Claire should do her jumping with me. I've said that from the beginning."

Her words stung like a hard rain striking into my eyes. I moved away from Daisy as far as the cramped trailer would allow. Had there been room to entirely turn away from Daisy, I would have shut the conversation down completely. I had, indeed, been an impulsive fool to reach out. Daisy had won; I had no energy to argue. Daisy and Claire's father were right.

Then Daisy spoke again. "Chancey, I've got to face the facts, too. Claire's father can't see the truth right now. I couldn't see it at first either. Gwen was right; Claire is your girl and you are her horse. You can't give up on her now. If you think you will be sold because of what happened today, I think you are underestimating Claire and her mother. If you are willing to give up so easily, then you are not the horse everyone's been trying to convince me that you are. And if they do sell you, then so be it. We will all go away one day."

Daisy leaned over the railing between us. "I know this, Chancey. In my lifetime, I have belonged with someone, and now he's gone. But it was worth it."

I rumbled to myself. I belonged with Claire; I could not deny that I belonged with Claire. I nipped at my belly, for the tangles would not relinquish their grip on me.

"Whatever happens, do not colic now," Daisy urged me.

I knew she was right. For no matter what the future held, every moment with Claire had been worth it. Though I wanted to acknowledge Daisy's kindness to me, I found myself unable to respond. My heart ached; the brick in my belly had increased in size. I could not reciprocate.

Daisy recognized my condition and did not require that I respond in kind. She leaned across the gate between us and blew on me. "Do not colic. Do you hear me? That little girl will need you when she recovers. Do not colic!" I knew that Daisy was correct: Claire needed me.

I do not pretend to have a medical understanding of how colic endangers horses. Nor am I well versed in its causes. I am well aware that colic is life-threatening. I know firsthand that it can arrive without warning, and that, even with ample warning, there are times when colic cannot be stopped. I can tell when it is imminent. Having colicked once in my life, I know what it is to face the possibility of such a painful death.

I was just a colt when my dam sustained a fatal injury; she had been defending *me*. A new mare had been introduced to our field and had challenged my presence there. Dam suffered greatly from a break in her shoulder. She could not have recovered. I know this now. Though I have lately heard of a horse that recovered from such a break, after surgery, it was not even a consideration those many years ago. I was a colt and I could not save Dam. Nothing could have saved Dam. My dam was resting in the field, stoically accepting her pain, waiting until they could come to take her away, as she knew they would. I stood vigil, protecting her as she had done for me so many times.

Dam knew that Monique would soon come to put an end to her suffering, and my dam was accepting—I think, grateful. The other mares visited Dam. One by one, each of them closed their eyes and whispered a final blessing across Dam's face. Even as the last mountain breeze she would feel waltzed around us, I begged Dam not to leave me. I was just a colt.

My dam did not turn back once Monique arrived to take her from the field.

"Come on, Starry; let's go now." Monique spoke tenderly to Dam. I whinnied and paced the fence line, urging Dam to turn around. I stood at the gate calling for her to look at me once more, for I knew if she did, she would come back to me. Though in grave pain, Dam walked on with Monique as if she were only going to be shod and then return.

I cried out for Dam morning and night, all the while fasting from food and water, so badly did I wish her with me. I was presently seized with a pain tangled deeply in my bowels. The knot clenched its grip on me forcefully and repeatedly, until I too lay down, ready to accept the consequence. I was just a colt.

I yearned for my dam; I lay down in the spot where she had lain. The grass was still matted from her weight, and something of her smell lingered there, too. I closed my eyes and wished for Saddle Mountain to bend over me and swaddle me so tightly that I would disappear into it forever. But mountains do not bend.

I writhed in the wet grass until finally I heard, "Get up." The mares had come to me, but they did not whisper their last blessings.

"Get up, Chancey. Get up and walk," they ordered me.

By turns, the mares pushed me up to my feet and, in pairs, boxed me between them. The mares tended to me by forcing me to stand up and move about until the tangled knots passed through me. I soon drank and ate again. But I was not the same. I was just a colt when my dam left and I colicked. I had not expected to ever love or depend on another as I had my dam. But I had not yet met Claire.

Returning from Tamworth Springs, I fought against colic for the second time in my life. I badly needed relief from what had ahold of me, just as badly as I had needed relief as a colt. I told myself that I would roll just once, just once for a second of peace. I dropped to my forearms. No sooner had I given my mind over to this urge than did the sky open up with such a forceful rain and wind that I instinctively rose to seek shelter in the run-in. Finding it crowded with the other geldings, I moved on, for upon seeing me, Dante pinned back his ears and would not allow me to enter the shelter.

There was one spot in my field, from which if I stood just so with my head held rather up, I could see the entire line of Saddle Mountain. Being that the spot is high on a hill in the far corner of my field, it took some effort to reach during the storm. It was there that I gave up. For the second time in my life, I then gave in to colic. Its grip was too tight; I could do nothing but roll and seek relief. Either the tangles would pass and I would live through the pain, or the tangles would win and I would die alone in the storm. I dropped to the ground and opened my belly to the sky. This time, there were no mares to tend to me. There was only the wind and the rain. Just as before, Saddle Mountain waited for the colic to run its course in me.

My mind began to create nonsense out of the wind. "Get up," I heard. Certain that my mind had now joined my eyes in a state of decline, and this voice was mere evidence of a new impairment, I whinnied to drown out the voice.

"Get up! Get up!" I heard the demand again, only in a much louder and firmer tone than either the mares of my youth or than I supposed my own confused mind might urge.

Softer now, more like a whisper in my ear, it was the Belgian, Macadoo, who called to me. "Get up and walk, friend." He pushed me up with his big head, and together we paced the hill in the pouring rain. Stu tried calling us in from the storm with grain buckets; Mac refused to leave my side, saying only, "I have been where you are, afraid and unsure of tomorrow. We will walk through the night together."

Through the storm we walked; I fought off the urge to fall to the ground and roll. We could not see Saddle Mountain through the sheets of rain. The wind threw branches and sticks to our feet, but I did not drop. The rain quickly filled the dry ruts in the field, and new rivers rushed down all around us. At times, the field turned so thick with mud that we sank down to our fetlocks. Still, we kept moving. Mac would not let the colic win.

When the danger of colic had passed, Mac and I stood together under the row of cedars at the fence line, waiting for the morning. I felt thirsty; I grazed on the wet grass and it caused no cramping or pain. Mac detected that some anxiety still lingered.

"What is it, friend? Why are you afraid?" he asked.

"I am not afraid. I am not afraid of hunger or cold or being beaten. I am not afraid anything. I am an Appaloosa; have you forgotten?"

Mac nuzzled me as a mother would do. "Chancey, it's me." He asked the question again, "Why are you afraid?"

I considered resisting Mac, but thought the better of it, for the Belgian had saved my life. As surely as the mares had saved me when I colicked at Dam's death,

Mac had saved me when I colicked at the thought of losing Claire.

I decided to speak the truth. "I am old, Macadoo. I am old and have been called dangerous for all to hear by Claire's father. He has even publicly called for my sale. I am afraid of myself. I am afraid to go back to that barn. I am afraid of Lynchville. I fear going blind; I fear I will forget the blue mountains."

Mac tossed his head back and forth. "My friend, you are carrying a great burden. Why don't you set it down now? There's no need to clutch it any longer. Have you not noticed? You live among friends now. You are loved."

I dropped my head to the ground, for the weight of these worries did, indeed, feel heavy. We grazed in silence under the stars. The force of the storm had moved farther south. From our hilltop we could appreciate its beauty as we watched it circle around the valley.

"Did you mean to hurt Claire?" Mac asked me.

"I am bound to Claire forever," I answered. "I would never hurt Claire."

"Do you enjoy jumping? Is that your purpose in life?"

I had never considered such a question. I ate some more grass; I was hungry. I knew not to eat too much until I could drink water and pass a normal stool.

I answered, "I love Claire, and Claire loves to jump. I'm not a jumper; it hurts me to jump. I love the open field. I can see better there, and my other senses can more easily help out. I love to teach. When a student is open, like Claire, I do love to teach. I love these blue mountains more than anything, besides Claire. Claire wants to be a teacher, you know."

Mac tossed his head, then touched my neck. "Well, there you are, Old App. You must stop jumping right away. Do not spend another moment jumping, for every moment jumping takes you further away from your purpose of teaching and showing students the joys of riding in these mountains."

I will admit that the burdens that had locked my stomach so tightly and forced me to the ground now vanished. I passed a very satisfying round of gas. Mac grazed beside me as if all had been happily resolved.

"Mac, what if the father is right? What if they sell me?" Mac looked up at me with a mouthful of grass. Our field was so wet from the storm that a foam of grassy residue had formed around his entire muzzle.

"Chancey, I have gone to auction twice in my life, yet I stand here before you a horse fulfilled. Both times, I endured and witnessed beatings by ignorant men. The first time, I was a yearling and had no one to protect me. Hundreds of others were lost to kill buyers in an instant. Despite their fine breeding, many finer than I, they were sold at a price measured per pound. Do you know what that means?"

I did not respond for I knew well the answer. I walked away from Mac to the other side of the hill, following the track of the storm below us. Mac followed me.

"They were eaten, Chancey. When the value of a horse is measured in his weight, Chancey, by the pound, it means he will be eaten. I was sold to a gentleman farmer, a gruff old man with a kind heart and a bad leg, for one thousand dollars flat. I survived. I am blessed and haunted by it daily. I had only a vision, placed on my heart by my mother, of a greater purpose for my life. Had I fought them at auction, I would not be here. Had I given myself over to them completely at auction, I would not be here. Acceptance is not the same as giving up. You seem to be giving up."

"But I am old. At auction, I would surely be sold for meat." I quivered at having finally named that which frightened me the most. Mac lost his patience with me. He reared up slightly.

"You must lead Claire and her mother to a new vision, Chancey. What is it that you want? Jumping is but one way to be a girl's horse. Has the father the final say in this matter? At the show, what did Claire's mother say about all of this?"

I thought back to Tamworth Springs. Mother was so quiet and lost in Claire's injury that I had lost her in my own recollection of the day. Claire's unconsciousness and her father's condemnation of me as a dangerous horse had overshadowed Mother, who in her grief, I now recalled, had spoken to me as the judge led me out. I tried to remember.

"Yes," I finally told Mac. "Mother did speak to me. She told me something very important. She whispered to me, 'You belong with us; don't ever forget that.'" Mac whinnied at me. "And I seem to have forgotten right away."

"Take heart, Chancey. Your work here is not completed. Only now are you ready to begin."

I stood with Mac in the gelding field that night and did not sleep at all. Claire did not come the next day, or the next, or the next, for her recovery took some time. While I waited, I forced myself to return to Mother's words—"you belong with us"—each and every time I became anxious.

Though neither Claire nor I realized it, the calamitous jump at the Tamworth Springs show would be our last jump together for some time. While our love for each other would grow deeper and stronger, this aspect of our working—training together as a hunter team— had come to an end.

## ★ CHAPTER FOURTEEN ★
### *Ode to Joy*

A week or more had passed, yet Claire still had not returned to the barn, nor had I any word of her condition. One afternoon, Mrs. Maiden came to me. She related to me that Claire had suffered a concussion, and though Claire was expected to make a full recovery, she would not be fully well for several more weeks. Mrs. Maiden's voice cracked when she spoke, and thus I could tell that she had been worried, too.

Though still under her doctor's care, Claire successfully prevailed upon Mother to bring her to the Maury River Stables just to see me. Claire insisted that the doctor's order of no riding did not mean no visiting. Tenderhearted Mother not only allowed Claire this occasion, but she believed that a visit would hasten Claire's recovery. This was reported directly to me by Mrs. Maiden, who not only informed me of Claire's impending visit, but showed me a great kindness by taking the time to groom me in preparation.

I appreciated this kindness very much, not only because it helped me to feel my very best for Claire, but also because it was the first time that Mrs. Maiden had expressed a true fondness for me. Make no mistake: the care that I had received, and receive to this day, was expression enough of Mrs. Maiden's deep love of all horses. But our grooming time, as we both waited for Claire and Mother, was Mrs. Maiden's first real display of personal affection for me, Chancey.

Mrs. Maiden set my brush box beside my front feet; it will come as no surprise to those familiar with the habits of girls that the brush box Claire had chosen for me was also purple. Starting on my left side, Mrs. Maiden began to brush my coat, talking to me the entire time. I enjoyed the sound of her voice, not just for what she told me, but for the fact that even though I could not see her, I could feel her at my left side and so never felt surprised at any action that she took. Mrs. Maiden is a kind woman, but she does not always feel as relaxed as she did on this morning. Understandably, with her great responsibilities of providing safety and protection to children and horses, as well as a few barn mothers like Mother who ride, she is often too preoccupied to relax.

With the same warmth that she uses only for the very youngest of her pupils, Mrs. Maiden said to me, "Claire's on her way, handsome boy. I know you've missed her. Claire's mother thinks a short visit will help her feel better."

Mrs. Maiden used a soft brush to clean my face; I closed my eyes and let the dirt fall from them to the floor. She lowered her voice and, touching my cheek, spoke again. "You know, sometimes little girls are hurt more inside than outside after a fall like Claire's. I bet her mother's right: a visit with you is probably just what she needs."

Mrs. Maiden fluffed my forelock and tucked our third-place Walk-Trot ribbon into my halter. Standing there in my room with the late afternoon sun streaming in the window and resting on my crest, I gave thanks for Claire's health and the many days we would have together.

Claire appeared at the door to my room just as Mrs. Maiden finished up. "You're gorgeous, Chancey! Did you get dressed up just for me?" Claire asked me.

Before I could manage any kind of an answer, Mrs. Maiden blurted, "Claire! You sure didn't get dressed up for Chancey. You're in your pajamas!"

Claire seemed not to hear Mrs. Maiden, for she did not answer her but threw her arms around me. "Oh, Chancey. I missed you so much. I don't even remember what happened the entire day. Mother said we got third place in the Walk-Trot class."

Noticing the ribbon, Claire observed, "The yellow ribbon looks pretty on you." She took the ribbon in her hands and confided in me, "I don't remember anything about the show. I only know I fell because Mother says so. I'm sure it was all my fault. Don't worry, boy, we'll be riding again soon. Mother and the doctor won't let me jump for a while. But we'll be together soon, I promise."

Daisy was right; Claire harbored no blame or resentment about the accident. Had my Creator given me tears to cry, I would have shed them all at that moment, so relieved was I that Claire did not intend to give up on us. Mother, I was also relieved to observe, seemed to share happiness at our reunion.

I listened closely to Claire's voice, as she told me how we would win our next show. She continued planning and dreaming of how high we would be jumping by the end of the year. I listened, but did not allow myself to dream with her. Claire rested her head on my shoulder and told me, "Chancey, you are everything I've ever wanted in a pony. Thank you for trying so hard, and for always being here for me."

Mother interrupted Claire's dreamy plans. "Claire, when you do return to jumping, we can't ask Chancey to jump with you again." Claire stopped breathing.

"Wh-what? But he's my pony. I don't want to ride anybody else, just Chancey." I moved closer to Claire, for I felt this same wave of sickness myself.

"I know, sweetheart. We have to honor Chancey and recognize his strengths and talents. It hurts him to jump. He tries so hard because he loves you so much, but it's not easy for him. To ask Chancey to jump higher and higher because you want to jump higher and higher is very unfair and very unkind. And one day, it could be very dangerous for both of you."

"Oh." Claire leaned into me. She rested her head on my shoulder and smelled me. "Oh." Claire nuzzled her face in my coat.

She began to cry. "D-D-D-D-Dad said we're selling him. I'll run, run, run away if we sell Ch-Chancey."

Claire clung to me and cried, hiding herself in my neck. "Please, Mother. Let me keep him. We don't have to j-jump. I love him so much. We can trail ride. I can practice my dressage. I can take him on a hunter pace. Please, he can do so many things."

Mother wiped Claire's face. "Claire, we will never sell Chancey. He is our family."

Claire laughed out loud and began crying again. I pressed my head close to my girl's heart and at the same time, flicked Mother with my tail.

Mrs. Maiden laughed, too. "Chancey is an amazing horse, Claire. He's just not a jumper, that's all. But he has so many other talents. When you're all better, you and I will find the perfect job for Chancey. In the meantime, let me take care of him and let your mother take care of you. Is that a deal?"

Claire hugged Mrs. Maiden, then Mother. "Deal." She nodded.

"Claire," Mrs. Maiden said, "let's turn Chancey out for the night. Would you like to lead him?"

Claire nodded furiously. "Could I?"

Then, as if it had almost slipped her mind, Claire asked permission to do something quite different. "Mrs. Maiden, I brought my violin to play Chancey a song. I've been practicing. Will that be OK?"

"What a nice idea, Claire—horses love music. In fact, why don't you go on and take him out to the gelding field and play there so Chancey and all of his friends can enjoy it?" Mrs. Maiden smiled.

Claire led me out to the field, with Mother following behind us. I noticed then that Mother held in her hands a black bag of sorts. As the three of us approached the gate, Dante, Napoleon, and Mac crowded the fence to greet Claire. Daisy, Princess, and Gwen all cantered along our adjoining fence line to greet her. I was not the only one who had missed Claire.

Dressed in her pajamas, Claire looked very much smaller than I had remembered. As is often the case after a storm, the entrance to our field was a mud pit, made worse by Dante's incessant pacing back and forth, guarding the gate, presumably against some unseen enemy. Claire and Mother seemed oblivious to the condition of the field and to their own ill-suited attire.

I stuck close to Claire as she unbuckled my halter. Mother opened the black bag and handed Claire what I presumed was the violin. I remembered how Claire had told me of her music when we first met. I nickered for Claire to show me the instrument.

Sensing my curiosity, Claire held the violin out to my right eye for inspection, for Claire was well aware not only of my blindness in the left but also of the narrow blind spot directly in front of my nose. Then she lifted the violin to her chin and with a stick of sorts began drawing out a low, sweet sound. I moved in closer to Claire's playing arm. She paused and encouraged me to thoroughly examine the stick.

"Chancey, this is called a bow," she instructed me.

With the ability to draw such rich notes from a hollow, wooden box, I should not have been surprised to find, as I was, that the stick, or bow as Claire called it, was strung end to end with strands of horse tail. I blew onto it.

"You're such a smart pony, Chancey. Of course, you're right. The bow is made from horsehair. So you see how horses and people make music together?" I nickered at Claire, encouraging her to continue playing.

My girl closed her eyes and brought the violin to her chin once more. I found that the notes appealed not only to me but, as Mrs. Maiden had predicted, to all of the geldings. All of us encircled Claire and Mother, getting as close as possible so that we could hear and see the fine gift Claire brought us.

I noticed that almost directly behind me, even the mares had lined the fence separating our two fields. They had stopped gossiping and gathered around to listen. I turned my head slightly toward the mares, to encourage them to come even closer, yet remain quiet. I am always amazed, and grateful, at the connection Claire and I have and credit the depth of this connection entirely to Claire's open heart and keen skills at observation. She saw, or felt, me indicate direction to the mares and ever accommodating and while continuing to play, Claire walked closer to the mares' fence so they, too, could share in the sweetness.

The geldings and I moved with Claire, as she now played to nearly twenty horses. We remained quiet, hoping that our stillness might consent Claire to play on. She played for us, without interruption, through many songs, occasionally asking Mother's advice as to which tune should be played next. Finally, Mother indicated to Claire that the time had come to leave.

Claire is as gifted in the art of managing Mother as she is in riding or playing music. She pleaded, "One more song, okay? What should I play?"

Mother indulged her without any sign of irritation or impatience. "Okay, one more song, Claire. Play 'Ode to Joy'; you've been working hard on it."

Again, Claire closed her eyes and poised her elbow in the air while she took in a deep breath. The cedar and river birch, all of us in the field, reached out to the sun, now falling behind the blue mountains. As Claire's bow pulled across the strings, the sun made one last rally, splashing our field with its easy afternoon light. I leaned in closer to Claire, grateful that she had not been irreparably harmed by the accident, and grateful that she was standing here with me. The storm had indeed passed; I wished for this song never to end.

When Claire finished playing, all of us remained standing near her, wishing, I think, for one more song. She handed the violin to Mother, then walked back to me, her pajama pants covered in mud. She stroked my neck; I felt content to be near her.

"Chancey, I have to go now. I love you, pony. I'll be

back soon, when I'm all better." Claire kissed me on my cheek, as little girls are fond of doing to horses.

Then she ran to catch up with Mother. Mother protectively slipped her arm around Claire's waist; Claire pressed her head into Mother's arms and leaned full into them. Mother nuzzled Claire's face, then opened the gate. I watched them walk all the way to the barn. Claire turned back several times to wave and blow me kisses. I nickered good-bye as she and Mother disappeared into the barn. Then, from the barn, Claire turned back once more and shouted to me, "I love you, Chancey! Sweet dreams!"

I was glad that we were still on evening turnout. Once the weather turned cold for good, we would again spend evenings in our rooms. The early autumn stars came down so close to the field, I felt sure that, from my spot on the hill, if I stretched up just a bit more, I would find myself among them, and perhaps I might find Dam there, too.

I stood all night watching for just one fire star and fell asleep waiting. No stars raced through the sky. Instead, the stars gathered close around me and held me in my sleep. When I awoke, in the morning, I understood. Dam had long ago told me that the stars said something special was planned for me. Finally, I understood.

In the morning, the gelding field looked very much the same as it had every day before, green and open with steps of granite boulders rising to the blue mountains. Napoleon was hiding under the cedar trees at the fence line; I could see his fat legs sticking out from under the branches and his long, blond tail sweeping the grass. Dante paced the gate, waiting for more hay to come. Mac grazed beside me, passing over the chickweed in search of any remaining clover. The mares were fighting over the morning's hay.

The world had not changed overnight, but I had. I had felt outcast among people and horses for much of my life. Even so, I had devoted twenty years to teaching. I had developed a strong habit of showing up and carrying on even though I hurt, even though I could no longer see well. Claire had shown me the most important lesson of all—that love grows when you give it away. Now, at last, I was ready to accept my calling. An extraordinary new beginning lay only a few months ahead for Claire and me, and it began with a gunshot.

## ✴ CHAPTER FIFTEEN ✴
# A Bombproof Pony

G uns don't frighten me, though I am aware of their capacity to harm animals and people. While I have no firsthand knowledge of a horse being mistaken for a deer, there are certain seasons when the threat does exist. It is uncommon for hunters to shoot near horses or cattle, so if we remain in our fields, we remain safe. The deer, of course, know this undisputed rule and thus often does, and occasionally bucks, will seek refuge among us. I can't say that I blame them at all. I might well be terrified myself if every second of daylight brought the threat of armed pursuit with intent to kill me.

Here at the Maury River Stables, Mrs. Maiden runs a special type of riding school, which she calls therapeutic. This school is indeed therapeutic for all involved in its operation, though I believe that the term *therapeutic* refers to the needs of the students enrolled. Mrs. Maiden chose me for the program not long after a rather disturbing incident in the gelding field one morning during the deer-hunting season. No one was hurt, and the day turned out quite well for me and opened the door to a future with a purpose so rewarding that I could not have imagined it for myself.

Before I describe my display of courage that drew Mrs. Maiden's attention, I must explain that I had encountered hunters and their weapons on two prior occasions. Both occasions, no doubt, drilled into me the response that Mrs. Maiden had found so admirable.

I first witnessed the power of guns at Monique's barn during the deer-hunting season some years ago. Monique was born with a good deal of fight in her; if she were a mare, she would undoubtedly be the boss. I admired this quality and sometimes felt that she recognized a bit of herself in me, which, despite a somewhat difficult two decades together, contributed to our long union. I remember one morning a deer herd, having been driven out of the forest by hunters, arrived at the mare field seeking asylum. Half as many men as deer soon followed and took it upon themselves to set up on

Monique's land in order to run the deer out of the field, in spite of clear trespass notices along the tree line.

Not surprisingly, Monique directly confronted the party of hunters, who had arrived with no shortage of guns or egos. It was an easy enough confrontation to predict, knowing Monique's strong distaste for hunters on the eastern side of her property. It should be noted that for many years, Monique granted exclusive rights to an older gentleman and his grandson to hunt the western side of her property with no restrictions save one—to give up the chase, even if in hot pursuit, if it meant coming into any of the fields with horses standing. I relay that to establish that, in fact, Monique held no prejudice against hunters, but did hold a strong prejudice about hunting her land without permission, especially too near her mares.

As Monique approached the hunting party, with commensurate gun and ego in tow, she neither flinched nor hesitated. She walked with sure stride, her gun pointed toward the ground, to the truck where the hunters had gathered. I was able to observe the incident, as the entire scene unfolded where the mare and gelding fences converged. Monique asked the hunters to leave, explaining that not only were they trespassing, but they were frightening her mares. The hunters laughed. I shook my head at their underestimation of Monique.

Monique did not laugh, but demanded that they

vacate her property immediately. There was no stutter in her voice; no syllable remained in her throat. One of the hunters adamantly claimed his right to engage because of hot pursuit. At that, I distanced myself from the dispute to create a safety buffer between us. The other geldings and mares followed suit.

Monique pointed her gun to the sky and fired it, startling the mares, the deer, and the hunters, who promptly left. No one was harmed, and our fields soon returned to normal. Thanks to Monique and her gun, we did not have such trouble again.

I have witnessed Mrs. Maiden make good use of her gun as well, again in defense of mares. It is here that I must stop and share my opinion that if Mrs. Maiden, or Monique for that matter, had considered placing a stallion, or even a strong gelding, with the mares, there might be no need for such protection, as that is the role of a strong male. I digress.

Though coyotes are not native to Rockbridge County, or the blue mountains, they have immigrated here and seem intent on settling. Horse farms, such as the Maury River Stables, haven't as much to fear from these rascally canines as do our neighboring cattle and sheep farms. Coyotes will, on occasion, however, intrude upon our mares, just for sport, I believe. This doesn't happen often, and again the placement of a strong male could deter this kind of taunting. Often, once the mares have banded together and threatened death by stomping, the coyotes will leave of their own accord.

Only once have I seen a coyote fail to respond to well-directed kicks and bites from our mares. That coyote, foaming at the mouth, met his death quickly, though I doubt painlessly, by the hand of Mrs. Maiden. She was alerted to the security breach in the mare field by my desperate calling to her. Upon seeing the coyote tormenting the mares, Mrs. Maiden retrieved her shotgun and, without a trace of fear, marched into the mare field, yelling at the coyote to distract him.

Though not all coyotes are call-shy, not even the most curious, if sound of mind, would have mistaken Mrs. Maiden's vocalizations for anything other than a threat. In the case of our rabid coyote, Mrs. Maiden's yelling had the effect of causing the coyote turn to away from the mares and set his course upon her.

Daisy and the mares cowered in the far corner of their field; Mrs. Maiden stood in the middle of the field, yelling and cursing the coyote. The words that shot out of Mrs. Maiden's mouth are the same words forbidden around the barn. I have seen Mrs. Maiden discharge from her employ more than one foulmouthed, defiant stable hand for such conduct as she displayed toward the coyote. Mrs. Maiden fired off every one of those words, and, indeed, her projectile of cursing seemed to draw the coyote closer to her, which was, of course, Mrs. Maiden's intent all along.

When the beast reached a proximity of about six paces—though you must understand that I am as poor a measurer of distance as I am a keeper of time—Mrs. Maiden simply aimed her gun, cursed at him one last time, and shot him between the eyes. The coyote may have yelped; I can't be certain of it. I am certain that a follow-up shot was unnecessary.

So, you see that I had twice witnessed the power of guns, and their usefulness, in times of danger to horses and people. I had not expected that the firing of gunshots would have led to a new and rewarding career for me. At my age, not much startles me, gunfire included, and that is what led to my recruitment into a new position at the Maury River Stables.

On the day of which I speak, three deer were grazing in the gelding field with us, enjoying quiet refuge from the forest full of hunters. The deer—two does and a young buck with perhaps half a dozen points on his antlers—behaved as if siblings. I had waited patiently for two seasons to lay eyes on the buck; his presence in the blue mountains was well known, for he was an albino, like me.

One should never really be surprised at the exquisite beings that are born of the blue mountains. The does who accompanied the buck seemed oblivious to his unusual coloring and unaware how his presence made them all stand out. Stu, who is a devoted hunter, had himself spoken reverently of the albino buck, whom he had seen and had opportunity to kill but, fearful that taking a pure-white deer might render him cursed, could not bring himself to fire upon. I wrongly assumed that all hunters believed, as Stu, that when our Creator grants us the privilege of sharing our space with a fine and rare creature, such as the white buck, the appropriate response is reverence. I believed the albino buck to be safe within our fence line.

I heard, then saw, on my right, four hunters crouched at the back fence, guns drawn. When I saw them so near our field, I believed they would refrain from opening fire, as the trajectory would have endangered the geldings. They readied their weapons. I lifted my head and turned my right eye more toward them to be sure that I had seen accurately. I confirmed their position and subtly, with only a slight movement of my head, relayed the location of the hunters to the three deer, out of courtesy.

My warning immediately sent the two does racing toward the safety of Saddle Mountain. The white buck remained with us. I moved between the hunters and the buck, though I failed to fully conceal him from the hunters' line of sight. He was too precious for me not to intervene; I expected the hunters to walk away.

What happened next shocked me; I have never known men to shoot so near horses. These men seemed oblivious to us geldings and irreverently unconcerned with the albino. Shooting rather recklessly into our field, they opened fire on him. This close-range firing caused great alarm among the geldings; all but Mac and I stampeded to the southern side of the fence. Fearing for their lives, ten geldings tore down the fence and galloped toward the Maury River, away from the hunting party. The buck took cover within the stampede and all escaped, unharmed.

Only Mac and I remained in our field. We called for Mrs. Maiden, who came quickly with Stu. Mrs. Maiden and Stu pieced together the chain of events quite accurately and with great speed. Wasting not a second, Mac escorted Mrs. Maiden and Stu to the fence, where they rightly observed that it been torn apart in a surge of fear by all of the missing geldings. While those three inspected the fence, I walked to the spot where the firing had begun, seeking any evidence that might be helpful to their investigation. On the ground, I spied an item similar to the residue that was left on the ground after Mrs. Maiden killed the coyote; I believed it to be a shell.

Certain that my discovery was germane to the inves- tigation, I trotted over, nudging Mrs. Maiden to follow me back to the spot. As I suspected, the shell provided confirmation to Mrs. Maiden and Stu of the incident. They rightly reconstructed the event, though they mistakenly deduced that there must have been one deer in the field, having no way of knowing that, in fact, three deer had that day been saved. Feeling that this detail was not critical for the recovery of our fieldmates, neither Mac nor I wasted any energy on the great effort it would have taken, such as presenting the two with multiple sets of tracks, to correct the notion of a solitary deer. It must be said that Mac and I both ably directed them to every clue available, short of opening our mouths and speaking.

Before Mrs. Maiden set about the chore of bringing the ten escapees home, she turned to Mac and me and, with very apparent gratitude, gave us each a nice pat, saying, "Thank you both, my brave boys. You weren't afraid, were you?"

She turned toward the barn to retrieve lead ropes and grain to bring the geldings home. Then she turned back to me and said, "Chancey! I've got an idea! Would you like a new job? I need a good, sound horse—a bombproof horse—to help Mac, Gwen, and me teach in the therapeutic school. Ask your buddy Mac what he thinks. I'll ask Claire's mother."

This seemed a revelation as to how a new vision of belonging with Claire would come to pass. Claire and I had met just when each of us needed the other. Claire needed a companion to help her sort out her feelings and find her confidence at a difficult time in her family life. She needed a friend who would believe in her and give her the courage to be great and true to herself. And I had needed exactly the same. What we had already accomplished together was more precious than one hundred blue ribbons; I did not want to see that foundation erode over time because any future ribbons weren't the right color.

I faced the truth of the matter. Whether she knew it or not, Claire needed something that I could not give her. Claire needed to be a champion; she needed to win. Though I would have given up the last of my remaining eyesight for it, I was not the horse who could take Claire to the level that she was ready to achieve.

I suppose that I should have felt regret about this truth, but I did not. Had Claire grown tired of me or rejected me for another, stronger gelding, yes, that would have cut to my heart. But Claire would have gone right on training with me three times a week, taking me to little hunter shows, and cantering me through the mountains, without complaint. She would have kept cheering me on with every fourth- or fifth-place ribbon we brought home. In Claire's eyes, we were a team. Had either of us placed competition at the center of our friendship, I believe we would not have lasted together as long or as true as we have. From the beginning, there was something more in it for both of us. I hoped that Claire and Mother would agree with Mrs. Maiden and allow me to try this new endeavor.

# CHAPTER SIXTEEN

## *My Training Begins*

I felt it a great honor to have been recruited to serve alongside Mac. Although less than half my age, Mac agreed to act as mentor to me as I prepared to enter service in the therapeutic school.

Mac had worked in therapeutic service since he was purchased at auction by Mrs. Maiden for that very purpose. To Mac this was not a menial position; it was his life's work. He spoke lovingly of his students and cautioned that should I accept the opportunity offered to me, I could no longer save the best of myself only for Claire. If I were to become a therapeutic school horse, I must withhold nothing and give myself to every student as if each one were, in fact, Claire. "There must be no favorites, my friend. To succeed in this work, each must become your favorite," he advised me.

According to Mac, each of my students would need something different from me. While one student might desire to gain muscle tone in her back, which had been ravaged by a disease of the muscles, another might wish to increase concentration in order to find a moment of peace from acute misfires in his brain. Still another student might work on improving his gross motor skills, which had been slow to develop. Mac impressed upon me that I must be ready to love each of my new students as deeply as I had come to love Claire. I vowed to welcome each student just exactly as I had been welcomed and nurtured.

When I arrived at the Maury River Stables, I too was in desperate need of restoration. Mrs. Maiden devised a plan specific to my needs. We worked to manage the pain from my arthritis. We salvaged what we could of my eyesight and used a variety of techniques to help me find new ways to see. Most of all, I finally found purpose and joy in my life. It was no accident that Claire was assigned to oversee my nourishment back to health. Mrs. Maiden gave me Claire because Claire was the person I needed in order to become whole.

It would be the same in return with my new students. Mrs. Maiden, together with each of my students, or their families, would create a plan for healing and strengthening. Through barn skills and riding, we would work in the therapeutic program to nourish body and soul, just as Claire had nourished me. I gathered that for therapeutic riders, horsemanship was a means to restoration. Whether to body or soul, my job would be to help restore each of them. I was eager to get started.

Mac assured me that proper training would equip me with the skills that I needed. He warned that therapeutic service, while rewarding, was also challenging. The training program on which I was about to embark posed the first challenge for me to overcome.

Mrs. Maiden had recruited me into my new position fully aware of my age and my conditions. It was Mrs. Maiden who had first observed the tumors in my eyes. Of course, Mrs. Maiden had also witnessed my refusal to jump with Claire because of my increasing blindness. These facts did not diminish Mrs. Maiden's faith in me, but I believe these were cause enough to put me through an intensive training with Stu.

Stu's charge was to increase my capacity to remain brave and calm under any and all circumstances. Courage has never been lacking in my spirit, thanks to my exceptional breeding. My dam was not only the most striking Appaloosa I have ever known; she was also the bravest, most serene being that I have yet to encounter. Dam was my first teacher in matters of courage.

I am not frightened to hear the wind tearing through our forest, even when there are few leaves to soften its howl. I am not afraid of other horses, be they moody mares or scowling, hot Thoroughbreds. I don't spook or dash away at the sight of a red umbrella, as do some others. A chair that was upright yesterday does not shatter my confidence if it is upside down when I encounter it today. Nor do I bolt when an engine backfires. I dare say neither friend nor foe can detect fear in me, ever. This courage was the trait admired so by Mrs. Maiden on the day the hunters fired upon our field.

Tolerance was to be my lesson. I quickly deduced, from listening to Stu and Mrs. Maiden plan my course of study, that increased tolerance was to be the primary aim of my training. By eavesdropping, I learned that Mrs. Maiden doubted not at all my bravery or my ability. She wanted to increase my tolerance to be able to accept the often unpredictable, erratic actions of some therapeutic students. I further overheard that I would not be immediately placed into service as a teacher. I would spend the rest of the fall and all of the winter learning to welcome intolerable and unexpected stimuli. Stu was to be my teacher, Mac and Gwen my mentors.

In addition to being the barn manager and a trainer at Maury River Stables, I am of the opinion that Stu was Mrs. Maiden's special companion. On a number of occasions, how many I cannot accurately state, I witnessed with my own eye a physical closeness between the two, the likes of which I have yet to see between other people. Their intimacy rivaled that of Claire and Mother, but at the same time was very different indeed. Having observed Stu's capacity for tenderness, I placed my complete trust in him and, in fact, welcomed him as my teacher. I felt certain that Stu would allow no harm to come to me, if for no other reason than his profound devotion to Mrs. Maiden.

Like me, Stu also battled arthritis. The disease had rendered his hands so twisted that the act of buckling the girth around me was very nearly impossible for him to complete without assistance. Yet he never winced or cried out. I saw how he rubbed his hands when the task was done. In this way, too, Stu trained me, through his example, to better tolerate that which aimed to distract me.

I was not surprised to find that Gwen, the old Hanoverian, along with Mac, was a star in the therapeutic school. There was no gentler mare in all of Rockbridge County. More than once, hearing Claire singing in the mare field, I had trotted over and found Claire sitting in the grass with Gwen's big, warmblood head resting in her lap. Claire held no fear of Gwen, who at seventeen hands high is a great deal larger than I am. I never disturbed the two of them at such moments, nor did I allow them to detect me as I watched from behind the cedar clump in the gelding field. Gwen's gentle spirit was well suited for teaching, particularly in the therapeutic school.

Before we started our training, Stu tied my lead rope to the door of my room so that I was facing the indoor riding ring. He proceeded to bring Gwen into the middle. She wore no bridle or halter and could have bolted from him at the moment of her choosing; she did not bolt. She appeared bored. Her breath warmed the air and formed a cloud around her face as she blew toward Stu with her standard greeting of exchanging breath.

With no warning or verbal cue, Stu reached back to his belt loop, then threw open an umbrella directly into the old mare's face. She blinked at him once, but made no sound or movement. She did not spook. She stood square in the same bored way as she had started out.

"See that, Chancey, my friend? That's you when we're done," Stu told me. Then he reached in his pocket for a treat, which Gwen gladly received. Ultimately, I was to achieve this same level of tolerance.

My formal training consisted of repeated conditioning to every unusual, unexpected sight, sound, or feeling that Stu could imagine. Stu started our work together by crumpling paper bags near my ears and face. He popped balloons next to my ears. Had Mac not opened my heart to the higher purpose of this most irritating training period, I may well have been put off and refused to accept these distractions. Stu dragged ropes and twine across my withers and barrel. He waved the rope around my face and rear. I did not react.

With no evidence that I understood his words, Stu explained to me that each lesson was necessary to simulate sensations that I might encounter with my new students. Stu's goal was to condition me to expect anything. When I had passed each test, Stu always made his satisfaction known to me with the same three words: "That's right, Chance." I came to expect that hearing the phrase signaled that we were ready to move on to the next challenge.

Throughout the winter, we trained everywhere. Our lessons were held in my room, the indoor ring, the out-door ring, the cross-country field, and, if Stu desired maximum distraction on any given morning, in the mare field. I may be gelded, but the mares still distract me like no other living beings. All over the grounds of Maury River Stables we worked for two sessions daily, in the morning after breakfast and again at midday.

Claire came most every day after school. Gradually, we all but stopped our own equitation training in exchange for taking quiet afternoon trails together. The winter ground was hard and crunched beneath my feet; I did my best to keep Claire warm, though I did not mind the cold as much as she did. Some days we had no need to talk at all and would only walk through the many miles of hills or alongside the river. Other days, Claire gave me detailed reconnaissance from Stu and Mrs. Maiden about my progress as a therapeutic horse.

"I'm so proud of you, Chancey. Everyone is proud of you, especially Mother. She gets all choked up whenever Stu tells her about how well you're doing."

In time for my evening meal, Claire would walk me back to my room. "I love you, pony," she'd say. Often Claire would return more than once with an extra carrot or apple to place in my grain box.

Mealtimes and after dark were the only hours I spent in my room while I was training. I can't say that I missed my room during my training as a therapeutic school horse, for I did not. I desired to pass as many hours as possible outdoors while I could still see. I knew that blindness would one day close the mountains to my eyes for good, for cancer knows not compassion. I knew there would be enough time for standing in my room, one day.

In order to build camaraderie, Mrs. Maiden had relocated Dante to the other side of the barn and now cradled me between my two mentors, Gwen and Mac.

To further cultivate an *esprit de corps* among us, she had sectioned off a new field in order that we could establish an unbreakable bond that would carry over to our work with the students. As Gwen was the oldest and most experienced in the therapeutic school, she easily and without fight became the lead horse in our paddock. There were occasions when, because of the shared fence line, Princess still assaulted Gwen. At those times, Mac or I were only too happy to race to Gwen's aid and slam our back hooves into the fence with such force and reverberation that Princess would not only scamper away, but squeal, too, as if she herself were the injured party.

At night in our bordering rooms, we three would whisper until early into the morning. Gwen and Mac made me repeat to them each exercise and aspect of my training progress; they then explained to me its purpose and described what I might expect the next day. I had easily passed the first phase of my training; still, Mac said even more was necessary before I could begin my work with students. Gwen rightly foretold that Stu would introduce me to more unpredictable stimuli than simple bags or colorful balloons. Thus, I was not at all alarmed when Stu showed up for my lesson with a pack of beagles.

★ CHAPTER SEVENTEEN ★

*Canis Familiaris*

Though I had exhibited great courage, enough to be recruited by Mrs. Maiden, it would be another month or more before Mrs. Maiden actually allowed me to teach in the therapeutic school. This next phase of my training would test me to the limits and ultimately desensitize me to loud noises and erratic movements. All of my senses would be reconditioned for extreme tolerance. I would have to learn that I could not bolt or squat, rear or buck, in retaliation of any stimuli. I would learn to accept, as had Mac and Gwen, that neither fight nor flight could ever be an acceptable response for a horse in therapeutic service.

Stu arrived at my room with all of his hunting beagles at his side. He hoped that using his dogs in my training would speed my progress. During the deer-shooting season, I had seen the dogs out on several occasions. As was customary, Stu began our lesson by greeting me in my room and offering me a peppermint from his pocket. A young beagle, whom I had not seen before, showed great interest in the candy and snatched it out of Stu's hand before I could take it myself. Stu lowered his voice. "Tommy!" he scolded. "Tommmmmy, that's not nice."

The puppy dropped his head apologetically, leaving the candy on the ground. I quickly scarfed it up for myself. I sniffed Stu's jacket, certain that I detected at least one more candy piece. Stu reached in his pocket and then handed it to me.

"Chancey, meet the new pup. His name is Tommy. His Latin name is *Canis familiaris*. He's going to help us today. If you like him, I'll bring him with us every day." I lowered my head to see the young dog, whose only interest was how much horse dung he could eat. Tommy took no notice of me whatsoever.

"Tommy, meet Chancey," Stu continued. "His Latin name is *Equus caballus*. Chancey's studying to be a therapeutic school horse," Stu told the dog. He patted me on the neck and added, "You didn't realize that I know Latin, did you, Chance? It's always good to learn something new. Keeps you alive."

I blew on Stu, for even though I had no interest in Latin or beagles, Stu had won a secure place in my heart precisely because he credited me for having such interests. Tommy remained obsessed with the ground.

In the cross-country field, Stu and his unrelenting hunting dogs set to work on me. It must be noted that I was never in any danger or under a threat of physical harm from the beagles. The dogs did not bite or nip at me, and I returned the favor by neither biting nor nipping at them. They did annoy. The beagles jumped and yelped. They crawled under me and used my rear and chest to prop themselves on two legs. Stu seemed to find their behavior endearing. I did not.

To keep myself focused, I played a concentration game with myself during these arduous sessions. I set about documenting and remembering my home so that even long after I had completely lost my sight I would still remember the Maury River Stables. I tried to completely tune out the dogs by imprinting the details of my surroundings onto my heart. I stood in our field, with hunting dogs bounding all around me. I could just see the tops of the sycamore trees lining the left bank of the river. While the dogs set about distracting me, I turned my mind toward the Maury River, and Saddle Mountain just beyond.

I recalled how when I first arrived at the Maury

River Stables, I visited the Maury River often and cantered alongside it searching for some clue as to where the river had been or what it was rushing to find. After a rowdy storm, the Maury might flow muddy and fast, pulling downstream an entire chestnut tree, or some such debris, which it had ripped from the banks upstream.

While the beagles lunged at me and pestered one another, I listened for the river. I confess that a part of me desired to break from Stu's dogs and gallop toward the sloping river birch that in the dead of winter marked the Maury definitively with its bright white bark. I knew the beagles would stay right on my heels if I attempted such a break.

Only once during this daily practice did the beagles successfully break my concentration. We had enjoyed an unusually high occurrence of rain; I knew the river ran high and fast, for I had no trouble at all hearing it rush by us, beyond the gelding field. I judged the electric fence to be approximately three feet high. As a young horse, I had successfully cleared more than three feet, but only a handful of times, if that, since coming to the Maury River Stables. Both the cancer and the arthritis had by then contributed to the demise of my jumping career, but logic had no such hold on me that morning.

Tommy began jumping at my left side, and I could not ascertain his intent. Though he stood no higher than the top of my cannon bone, his vertical range reached much nearer to my cheek than I had expected. I felt Tommy there, bouncing up well past my forearm, but could not see him. I could hear the pup; it would have been impossible not to hear him. I could smell him, too, for this young beagle had no bladder control whatsoever and in his excitement, he covered my feet in the contents of his bladder more than once. Though it had been almost a year since my first tumor was removed in Albemarle, and I had by then grown accustomed to complete blindness in my left eye, I panicked that I could not see but only feel Tommy there at my side. I tried to ground myself with my remaining good eye.

Tommy then launched himself above my head. I cast about for the sound of the river. I was sure I could clear the electric fence. I flicked my tail at Tommy and began to dance. I pinned my ears back, a fair notice of warning. The young beagle continued, aware, no doubt, that he had gotten a reaction from me and from Stu as well. I lifted my front left foot and poised it there, giving Tommy one last opportunity to leave me alone. "Chance, you can do this," Stu urged. But it was too late; I kicked the little beagle away from me, not hurting him badly, mind you. Without question, if my intent had been to injure the pup, I would have done so with such might that little fellow would not have been able to run crying to his mother, as he did.

I knew my error straightaway and regretted it. I did not bolt to the river. I stood square in front of Stu, who just laughed. "Whoo, Chancey, he got to you. Tommy got to you."

Stu sent the dogs to the front of the field, where they obediently waited for him. He moved to my left out of my vision, and patted me on the neck. "It's your left side, I know. You've done a fine job compensating until now. Don't worry, Chance, don't worry." Stu did not sound disappointed but rather satisfied with what he had discovered about me. I hoped that my outburst toward Tommy had not eroded Stu's confidence in me.

I was comforted to walk with Claire that afternoon and relieved that she already knew about the incident with Tommy. Claire did not tack me up but walked me bareback up an old logging trail around the base of Saddle Mountain. Few leaves remained on the mountain and those that did swirled around behind us for the entire five-mile trail. We stayed inside the mountain, for neither Claire nor I dared to take on the frigid, unrelenting mountain air at the unprotected peak. On our return to the barn, Claire finally told me.

"I heard about that annoying puppy this morning. I don't blame you for kicking him. Don't worry; he's not hurt. Stu's not mad, either. He said every therapeutic horse he's ever trained has cracked with the beagles . . . except Gwen."

Claire patted my neck. "You're doing a good job, pony. Stu says you're one of the best."

Claire, Gwen, and Mac, between them, kept me motivated during my training. Without them, I would have easily become discouraged.

★ CHAPTER EIGHTEEN ★

## Equus Asinus

Mac predicted that my training would soon extend beyond the Maury River Stables onto adjacent properties. As ever, Mac was correct. Our lessons were no longer stationary, which Mac assured me was indicative of great progress in my training. Stu intended to introduce me to companions immensely more annoying than Tommy and the other beagles. In Rockbridge County, many people keep horses, and as they all ride and love the countryside, a strong tradition of courtesy use exists for the purposes of pleasure riding nearly every day of the year, except for those days when hunters are allowed in the woods.

For our first morning ride, Stu tacked me up quickly with only a bareback pad and a lead rope tied into reins. I am always overjoyed to ride without the bit in my mouth. I don't mind the bit so much in the hands of a rider as knowledgeable and kind as Stu or Claire. Claire and I often ride without a bit or saddle and I can say, with certainty, we both enjoy that very much. In the case of Stu, unlike some of my younger and more diminutive riders, his instructions to me through his legs and seat are straightforward and easy enough to follow that the additional aid of the bit is unnecessary. Stu is not a big man, by comparison to John the Farrier or Doctor Russ; Stu's weight, because it is well balanced and evenly distributed, actually gave me much confidence and security as we rode.

Stu led me away from Maury River Stables with great purpose. My nemesis from the cross-country field, Tommy, accompanied us. To my surprise, the puppy behaved more respectfully to me after I had kicked him. He stopped relieving himself on my feet, an outcome that was well worth the mild kick I had previously delivered. Having learned his lesson, Tommy ran beside me, always on the left and well away from my feet. His panting and yelping kept me aware of his position and served to mark the left edge of the trail. I found that by keeping an ear turned toward Tommy, I was able to use him as a guide on the trail. The willing pup kept alongside me; his presence kept me from stumbling into ditches or holes. I began to warm to his personality and could see why Stu was so fond of him.

We rode away from the Maury River. Our destination was Mrs. Pickett's farm, some distance from our barn, past a neighboring cattle pasture, through an over-planted pine farm, and across the paved street.

As we approached Mrs. Pickett's farm, we moved straight along the fence line at a nice working trot. Before I could see my distraction, I heard him. His coarse voice grated my ears so badly that Tommy's yelping would have soothed me. I wanted to bolt, not from fear, but to get some relief. The honking was not altogether unlike a horse, but not nearly as refined. It was not quite a neigh and definitely not a whinny. I wasn't frightened, just annoyed.

Stu kept me trotting, again keeping the fence on my right, which I greatly appreciated. The beast, upon seeing me, acted quite as if we were long-lost brothers. He magnified his horrendous noise tenfold, alternately begging me to break him out of the fence and pleading with me to jump over the fence to live with him. He professed to be a lonely soul, certain that I had been sent by our Creator in answer to his prayers.

I did not laugh when I saw him, for I know well the

feeling of being laughed at and would not wish that feeling on any fellow being. He stood on four disproportionately short legs with a barrel almost as wide as mine. He very nearly appeared to be a horse, but a most uncommonly exaggerated one. Besides his torturous voice, his astoundingly elongated ears were his most defining characteristic; they towered above his head straight up at attention. As I moved closer to him, I observed that his nose was nearly twice as long as my own. Indeed, I had to suppress my deep urge to laugh, for he was comical in every way.

As Stu had orchestrated this gathering, he introduced us formally.

"Chancey, my friend, meet Joey. This is Mrs. Pickett's new donkey, also known as *Equus asinus.* Y'all are kinda cousins, I guess, since you're both *Equus.*"

Joey seized upon the mention of a familial connection. He turned his ears rapidly to and fro, then rolled his eyes down to Tommy. He squeezed his oversize nose under the fence and said to the puppy, "Yes! Yes! We're cousins, you and I. Yes, we are."

Offended as I was at Stu's ludicrous suggestion of a genetic resemblance between Joey and myself, I was even more offended that Joey would feel elation at being related to a beagle, when an Appaloosa stood right in front of his eyes. I did not flatten my ears, though I most certainly wanted to do so.

Tommy furiously wagged his tail in circles at the donkey, eager to be adopted. Taking no notice of me, Joey invited Tommy into the family. "Hello there, little wagger. Hey, I have a tail, too. Look at my tail; look at mine!" Joey flicked his tail around for Tommy to see. Tommy barked and yelped to encourage his new cousin, *Equus asinus.*

I could take no more of their foolishness; I pinned my ears, showed the whites of my eyes, and whinnied sharply into the donkey's ear. Joey looked up from sniffing Tommy.

"Are you my cousin, too?" Joey asked me.

I then set the matter straight. *"I'm* Chancey, not him. He's not our cousin. He's *Canis.* We're *Equus."* Joey practically threw himself over the fence toward me.

"Oh, cousin! Oh, Cousin Chancey! I've been waiting for you to come. Please, don't ever leave again," pleaded Joey.

I had learned by then that the longer I held my curiosity on any new object in our lesson, the longer Stu would require me to spend on that lesson. Eager to be far away from my new cousin Joey, I feigned boredom by dropping my head to graze and passing gas. This technique proved itself as Stu picked up my head and with a squeeze of legs we set off again.

Joey begged us not to leave him. I promised we would return in the morning. Even as we cantered out of sight, Joey still called to me, "Come back! Hey, come back! There's nothing down that way but a mean, spiteful llama. Come back, cousin! Come back!"

Before we could move into a gallop, an ugly, shaggy animal with a neck longer than any I've ever seen, and even longer eyelashes, came running up beside us. I guessed this was the llama of Joey's warning. He did not appear to be mean, or spiteful, as Joey had suggested, just odd. I was most curious. As the fence line was still at my right, I was able to observe this striking animal more closely. Stu never changed his directions to me, so, lacking any perceptible shift in leg or hand, I continued to canter the fence line, with the long-necked animal and Tommy cantering along beside me. I felt the llama sizing me up with his eyes and nose. Had Stu given me room, I would liked to have shown that llama the impressive speed that Appaloosas are capable of reaching. Though the llama spoke not a word, the air between us smelled of tension.

I hadn't the chance to become too agitated, for Stu pulled me to halt. The llama halted as well. I was pleased when, at the end of the fence, Stu gave me my head to investigate. I am ashamed to say that after the long canter, I was shorter of breath than the llama, Stu, or Tommy.

Stu introduced us. "That's a llama, Chancey. I don't

know his name. I don't know his Latin name either. He belongs to Mrs. Pickett, too. We'll give him another race tomorrow."

I nodded to the llama. We stood face-to-face, yet the llama would not exchange breaths with me. I studied him carefully for some clue as to his rancid demeanor toward me.

This bushy fellow had no fine tail like mine, and really had practically no tail at all. Nor did he have any sort of mane. It struck me as especially odd that his ears stuck straight out to the sides horizontally, not elegantly tall, like mine. He was covered in a short, furry coat that made me so itchy my tail involuntarily flicked in a rhythm reserved only for the most persistent flies. Though he stood almost to my height, most of the llama's height was in his neck. I deduced that he weighed considerably less than I. In response to my greeting, the llama batted his long lashes, then proceeded to spit in my face. Then he turned his full attention to Tommy. I decided that Joey was the more tolerable creature of the two.

In the barn that evening, as I recounted the day's lesson to Gwen and Mac, I could see they were impressed with my advancement. Mac nodded toward the mares across from us. "See Princess?" Mac threw his head in her direction. "She came unglued at the llama on a trail ride last week. She nearly threw her rider and wouldn't go a step farther. The entire riding party had to turn around and come home."

Gwen leaned close to me and whispered through the bars separating our two rooms. "You won't believe this, but Dante is scared of the donkey."

I laughed. "He's frightened of our cousin Joey?"

"Shhh, he might hear you," warned Gwen. Then she continued, "It's Joey's voice that frightens Dante. He rears and bucks over there by Mrs. Pickett's. He won't go anywhere near Joey."

I cut a glance at Dante, our boss, who was too busy kicking his room door to bother with listening to us. Gwen nudged me with her nose. "And don't look at him either. Here, look at me."

I was encouraged by our conversation that evening that my formal training was coming to an end, and soon I would begin to work with students in the therapeutic school. I confessed that I was nervous. My training had gone well, but had it really prepared me for the dynamic, real-life world of being a school horse again—and in such a highly specialized school?

My mentors assured me that I would never be alone; I would work with my students in partnership with many people and other horses. Mac or Gwen would always be in the ring with me. Not only would one of my two good friends be there, but Mrs. Maiden or Stu would handle me directly for the duration of each lesson, and for added comfort and protection of the students, specially trained volunteers called sidewalkers would join me as well.

Macadoo explained that sidewalkers were required to complete a training program just as the horses were. While Stu handled the training of horse partners, Mrs. Maiden coordinated the training of sidewalkers. Each therapeutic student would be assigned two sidewalkers per lesson. The sidewalkers would attend to my students' equipment, teach them about grooming, and monitor things such as correct seat position and foot placement. Some students might require sidewalkers to hold them in the saddle and walk along the left and right side of me. Other students might need nothing more than praise and motivation. If I happened to spook—a highly unlikely scenario because therapeutic horses are dependable and unspookable—the sidewalkers would remove the rider, if necessary. If my student needed help steering, the sidewalkers would help steer. The sidewalkers would be there for whatever was needed during the lesson.

This was the first I had been told that I would work so closely with sidewalkers. My stomach rumbled. I wondered how well my sidewalkers would manage with my blind side, or if they would even welcome getting to know an old horse such as myself. My nervous stomach erupted into a very loose stool. I ignored my symptoms of anxiety; I did not share my concerns with Mac or Gwen, for I was determined to prove to myself and Mrs. Maiden that I was worthy of the therapeutic school. More than anything else, however, I wanted Claire to be proud of me. I wanted Claire, and Mother, too, to see that though I could not give Claire the championships she deserved, I was still a good, sound horse.

"Old App," Mac said one night after my last training session with Stu, "we've saved some very special news until now. We've all been saving a surprise for you. I didn't want to tell you until you had made it this far in your training program." Mac moved from his window to the wall between our rooms. Gwen came closer, too.

It was difficult to speak privately in the barn, for we had to speak in whispers. We had much freer conversations when we were turned out in the field; we all looked forward to the springtime, when we would be outdoors more. I put my ear to the bars between us to hear Mac's news.

"Your sidewalkers will be Claire and Mother." I wasn't sure I understood what Mac meant. Did he mean that I would not have to work with strangers? My family would be joining me in service to the therapeutic school? I leaned as close in to Mac as I could.

"What? Would you say it again, Mac?"

Gwen repeated Mac's news. "It's true, Chancey. Claire and her mother have been training with Mrs. Maiden while you've been training with Stu. I heard Claire say you weren't getting away from her so easily. They're going to volunteer with the therapeutic program, too. You three will be a new team. How do you like that?"

I nickered softly to Mac, then exchanged breaths with Gwen. Mac walked over to his window; I walked to mine and pushed it open with my nose. At that time, I was blessed that the vision in my right eye still allowed me a clear and fine view of the moon hanging full between Saddle Mountain's pommel and cantle, throwing off rays nearly equal to early morning sun. Mac and I did not speak; we stood in our stalls, both looking up at Saddle Mountain. I had worried about the sidewalkers for nothing.

By spring, Claire, Mother, and I were prepared to teach in the therapeutic riding school, together.

# CHAPTER NINETEEN

# Three Times Weekly

By the first day of spring, Claire, Mother, and I were working in the Maury River Stables Therapeutic Riding School. Three times weekly after Claire's school day had ended she, Mother, and I taught a lesson as a team. Though Claire was at that time only eleven, she had completed the required training and was considered a junior volunteer able to serve alongside Mother.

Our charges in the therapeutic school ranged in age from the very young, of perhaps five years of age, to much older, closer to the age of Mother. I found satisfaction and purpose in this work and felt that my entire life had prepared me to teach in this way.

My therapeutic students always greeted me with affection and treated me with the greatest respect. They often brought me drawings and paintings for my room; some gave me cookies and treats. Others, I was told, included me in their bedtime prayers, and it was for this that I was most thankful. To be so loved at such an advanced age as mine was a great motivator. Their devotion humbled me.

I returned their love fully and generously. Whether I was hot or cold, whether I was in pain or enjoying a respite free from pain, I welcomed every therapeutic student, every time.

Why some students attended the therapeutic school and others did not was not always immediately evident to me. True, for many of my therapeutic students, a physical impediment blocked their technical mastery, but that was truly the case with all my students, whether in the therapeutic school or not. Take Mother, for example: a deformity in her back impeded her technical mastery, and an unexamined fear in her mind kept her from pushing herself further. Yet Mother was not enrolled in therapeutic school as a student but as a sidewalker volunteer with Claire.

I gathered from Gwen and Mac that the therapeutic riding school served people of all ages who were in some manner wounded. Perhaps they had no use of their legs, which was easy enough to discern since in those situations, a chair with wheels carried them up a special ramp built to the height of a horse's back so that all transfers were made laterally. This removed the danger that could be caused by lifting a student up and over onto my back. Other students brought wounds that were more difficult to detect because there was no outward evidence.

I quickly observed that the most noticeable difference in most of my therapeutic students was that they possessed an uncommon openness and willingness in their hearts. I will take heart and loving-kindness over technical ability any day of the week—for a rider with an open heart allows the fullest possible joining up, whether galloping over the Maury River, slowly walking a figure eight, or merely standing in my room watching the blue mountains.

Before I started this work, Mac told me we could not play favorites in this job. I suspected Mac spoke from having learned from experience that such strong attachments eventually cause a degree of brokenness in the heart. I, however, am not ashamed to disclose that there were a couple of students to whom I was particularly partial.

One student, a girl named Kenzie, I learned after three lessons together, could not see out of either eye. At first, I had thought perhaps Mrs. Maiden had mistakenly placed Kenzie in the wrong program. She moved with such confidence and grace in the saddle and on the ground and with a heart as open and kind as any girl, save my Claire. I adored Kenzie; she was like a blast of spring, arrived in the dead of winter. Her blindness did not prevent her from placing her full trust in me or Claire and Mother, her sidewalkers.

Claire and Mother kept us moving as a team by acting as Kenzie's eyes and, of course, compensating for my own left eye. They guided us around the ring and over poles, or around a spiral of cones set up for bending practice. Truthfully, Kenzie had little need of sidewalkers in a traditional sense. Claire and Mother gave Kenzie no physical support. Nor did they make actual contact with Kenzie or me. They jogged or walked alongside me and used their voices more than anything— Claire instructing us and Mother encouraging us.

"A little more leg, Kenzie. Now close your hands around the reins, but don't pull back on them. Sit down and relax," Claire would say.

After trotting circles in our corners without breaking, Mother would applaud us both. "Beautiful, Kenzie! Beautiful, Chancey! Now enjoy this straightaway— you're doing great!"

Mrs. Maiden always kept the therapeutic horses on a lead line, for precautionary measures. After only a few lessons, Kenzie became such a proficient rider that Mrs. Maiden hardly worked at all. I listened for Kenzie's directions, and Mrs. Maiden kept the lead line slack. I certainly would have indulged Kenzie a bit more than my other students if she had squeezed her hands too tightly around the reins. Yet she held the reins with a light touch as if they were robin eggs in her palms. If, because of her blindness, Kenzie had fallen on my neck a bit more than my sighted students, I would gladly have tolerated her weight. But she kept her center of gravity fully aligned with mine.

Kenzie rode with an open heart. Like me, she used her ears, her nose, and every nerve in her body to work for her eyes. My role with Kenzie was simply to respond to her touch, her voice, and her feelings. When Kenzie brushed my body, I made a quiet, low sound of contentment so she could feel that I enjoyed her manner of grooming me. If Kenzie wrapped her arms around me for affection, I wrapped my neck around her in kind, so that she could feel my affection, too. In the saddle, I paid close attention to the directions of Claire and Mother as they instructed Kenzie which aids to deliver, so that at the slightest detection of effort on her part, I obliged. Kenzie showed me that eyes are but one way to see the world. She comforted me a great deal, and every time I spent an hour or two with Kenzie, my fear of losing my own sight lessened.

Zack, a boy student of mine, bore no evidence of

physical wounds at all, but even as he picked up the body brush to groom me, I sensed that his wound hid deep within his mind and so prevented him from enjoying or experiencing much of anything for more than the briefest measure of time. With Zack, my task was to reach deep enough into that wound and give it a soft enough interruption that it did not send Zack's sparks flying. With Zack, I strove to relax him enough that his concentration would increase over time.

Zack's nature was such that he took in too much information, too quickly, and then became paralyzed by a jungle of stimuli. When Zack started with me, he would regularly melt down, as Mrs. Maiden described it. I know that to a stranger looking at our progress, or perhaps trying to chart Zack's progression as a rider, it may have appeared that we were slow to advance. But I am proud to say that we made extraordinary progress together. Eventually, Zack could hold his mind quiet and groom my entire right side before he disengaged again and had to be redirected to the task by Mrs. Maiden. Frequently, Zack would stand near me and take in only the feel of my mane or the touch of my nose to his neck for some time before he became distracted again. It was several months before Zack made it out of my room and into the ring. To understand our accomplishment, you would need to feel what it is like to be Zack.

When we did begin our work under saddle, Claire and Mother had a much different role as Zack's sidewalkers than they did as Kenzie's. At our first lesson, Zack was frightened to be in the saddle; he screamed and thrashed around. He was unable, however, to calm his mind enough to get down or get help getting down.

"I want down! I want down! I want down!" Zack screamed.

I stood square; I did not dance. Tommy, who had been trying to stir up trouble in the mare field, heard the commotion and ran over to the edge of the lesson ring. I blinked my eyes at Tommy and pinned my ears back, warning him to stay out of the ring. I knew Zack didn't like dogs.

"Down! Down! I want down!" Zack began kicking his legs and pulling wildly on my reins in an effort to free himself from the saddle. There were too many places of connection: two stirrups, two hands on the reins, and several feet between him and the ground. Zack didn't know where to begin. Claire interrupted the boy's thought process.

Claire clapped her hands. "Zack!" Zack turned to Claire.

"Do you like ice cream? Chocolate ice cream?" Claire asked him.

He forgot that he wanted down. Mother lifted the boy out of the saddle and placed him on the ground beside her. I turned my head back to see if he was all right and touched my nose to his shoulder.

"Hi, Chancey." Zack waved at me. "I was way up there." He pointed to my back.

Claire held her hand out.

"Zack, come with me. We're going back down to the barn to teach you emergency dismount on a barrel. That way you'll know what to do if you ever freak out on Chancey or any other horse."

"Okay, Claire. What about the ice cream? Do we get ice cream after I learn emergency dismount?"

Zack never forgot emergency dismount and, in fact, he used it at every lesson. He said it made him feel like a superhero. Claire, Mother, and I learned to be on guard at any point in our lesson to hear Zack shout out, "Ready y'all? Emergency dismount!" I would halt immediately. Then Zack would fling himself out of the saddle, just as Claire had taught him to do that day in the barn. Mother was always there to spot him and give him an able assist to the ground. Mrs. Maiden learned to keep chocolate ice-cream bars in the freezer, for Zack always asked for ice cream after emergency dismount.

Once, after a lesson, I heard Zack's father say that the boy had brought home a B in one of his classes at school, which meant nothing to me in and of itself. But I saw Zack beam at his father's pride. I heard the child tell Mrs. Maiden, "Now, when I get overloaded, I think

of brushing Chancey. Then it's easier to calm down."
Zack has taught me that no achievement is to be over-
looked or undervalued.

Yes, Kenzie and Zack gave me many hours of satisfaction and joy. I eagerly anticipated our meetings each
week and was not surprised to find that I grew as much
as either child. I loved Kenzie and Zack very, very
much. Still, neither was my favorite. Two years would
pass before I would meet that student.

# CHAPTER TWENTY

# A Child Like Me

Trevor Strickler could see with his eyes perfectly well, excepting the long bangs that hung in his face, not unlike the unkempt forelock sported by Napoleon the Shetland pony. Trevor also was capable of a deeper, longer concentration than most adults whom I have taught.

Trevor was like me, only Trevor was not old, and his cancer did not take his eyesight first. His whole body was filled with cancer. A bit younger than my Claire, Trevor was, in his own words, "too old to be treated like a baby and forced to take riding lessons." My job with Trevor was to find joy. That was my sole task, to help my friend feel joy.

I could feel my own cancer, behind my eyes, growing deep within me, waiting, I believe, for my work to be done. I know that Mother and Doctor Russ had kept my cancer at bay for as long as possible. Over the past few years, I had submitted to eye surgery as a matter of routine, to remove the cancer not only from my left, but also my right eye. Doctor Russ confirmed that I was slowly losing vision in my right eye, but with surgery, he was able to slow down its pace. Doctor Russ regularly pointed out to Mother that I was, after all, an old horse.

When I first met Trevor, he wanted nothing at all to do with me or any horse. Though enrolled in the therapeutic school and assigned me as his horse, as he did not participate in lessons, there was no need for sidewalkers. In fact, Trevor refused to acknowledge me in any way. He would not pick up a brush or a currycomb. Mrs. Maiden, Trevor, and Trevor's mother would stand in my room for an hour, once a week, waiting for Trevor to show an interest. Trevor would stand with his back to us all, kicking the wood shavings against the wall of my room.

I ignored him because that is what he desired: to be left alone. Having turned my back on many, it's a gesture that I understand fully. When an about-face like Trevor's is deployed with such conviction, it is prudent to honor the request to be left alone. I did not judge the boy in his anger, nor did I take it as a personal affront. I

didn't feel the urge to defend myself against his out-
bursts, for they were directed at the wall, not me. Besides,
Claire was plenty equipped to defend my dignity.

Though Claire had advanced in her jumping and
dressage well beyond my abilities, she refused to give up
her riding time with me. Claire's attachment to me, and
mine to her, allowed us each to feel secure in pursuing
our separate paths confident in the knowledge that we
were eternally bound. I loved our work together in the
therapeutic school and our riding time in the mountains.

Claire and I had kept an easy routine of taking to the
trails in the afternoons. We often strolled down to the
Maury River in order to cool down from the hot afternoons. After wearing ourselves out in the water, Claire
would sit on my back drying off while I grazed the lush
banks of the river.

"See Saddle Mountain up there, Chancey?" Claire
would ask. "One day, I'll take you up there again. We'll
canter all the way to the top, then look out at everyone
we know. They won't see us or know where we are. It
will be just the two of us, looking out at the whole
world, together."

I did not doubt Claire that one day we would find
ourselves on the highest peak of Saddle Mountain. I
looked forward to that day and hoped it would, indeed,
come to pass. I had by then grown accustomed to Claire
riding many different horses and this did not concern

me or detract from my love for her, or hers for me. Claire and I had saved each other, and I knew, truly, that our love for each other grew even deeper as our training together came to an end.

I was happy that my therapeutic service did not supplant my time with Claire. Once a week, my trail time with Claire followed immediately after my lesson with Trevor, which could not be accurately described as a lesson, but more precisely standing-around-in-my-room time with Trevor. One afternoon, Claire arrived at the barn early, at the request of Mrs. Maiden. She had asked Claire to come out early to pick up registration forms for the Ridgemore Hunter Pace, a cross-country race of sorts that I very much hoped would be the event where Claire and I would finally win our first blue ribbon together, and my first blue ribbon ever.

Claire and I had not entered a competition together since Tamworth Springs. With Daisy, Claire had won every hunter show on the circuit. The pair brought home champion ribbons regularly, and Claire always came straight to my room afterward to tell me stories of the day. I did not miss the stress of hunter shows, and was glad that Daisy was the one to take my place. Daisy and I had come to appreciate each other; the mare excelled in hunter shows. Still, I longed to compete just once more with Claire and thought the hunter pace a perfect setting to do so.

Mrs. Maiden had convinced Claire that I would excel at a hunter pace. Though the course would include optional jumps, each jump would offer a go-around. Together, Claire and I would ride as a team over seven or eight miles of open pasture, up into the blue mountains, crossing over the Maury River several times. We would join with another horse and rider to form a team of four—two people, two horses—in a challenge to ride not the fastest, but the closest to the time the judges had determined to be optimum—a time that would not be announced until after the event had ended. The hunter pace was designed to test endurance, speed, agility, wit, and sportsmanship—all characteristics bred into me and highly developed among all Appaloosa horses.

Neither Claire nor I had dared utter aloud our hope that we might win the hunter pace, but we needn't, for it was there in both our hearts. Though the event was still several months away, Mrs. Maiden preferred her students to register early for purposes of scheduling trailerloads and finding substitute trainers to teach in her absence.

Claire picked up the form and, as was her routine, brought her tack to my room in preparation for the trail. There we all stood, Trevor, with his back turned; his mother, absently brushing my neck in the same spot over and over; Mrs. Maiden; and Claire.

Mrs. Maiden introduced Claire to Trevor and his

mother. "Trevor," she said, gesturing to the boy as if he were really listening, "this is Chancey's owner, Claire."

Then she told Claire, "Trevor rides Chancey every Friday right before you do."

Claire did not know, as did I, that it was perhaps not a lie, but at the very least an extreme exaggeration to state that Trevor had ever ridden me, for he had refused to even interact with me.

Mrs. Maiden seemed rushed. "Claire, I am kind of in a bind today with the farrier coming to shoe and the vet coming to give shots. Could you help Trevor tack up, please?"

Trevor's mother opened her mouth to protest, but Claire answered too quickly, "Sure!"

Mrs. Strickler placed a protective arm around Trevor's shoulder; he did not turn around. She smoothed the back of her son's shirt. She pushed his long bangs out of his eyes.

Mrs. Maiden took Trevor's mother by the elbow and escorted her out of my room, saying over her shoulder, "Thanks, Claire. I knew I could count on you."

Claire moved toward Trevor as if it were perfectly expected that he would be tucked into the corner of my room.

"Come on. I'll help you." Claire did not know that Trevor had made a practice of angrily kicking my wall for several weeks in a row. I could have told her that he had no intention of tacking me up.

Trevor lashed out at Claire. "I don't need your help! And I don't want to ride your stupid horse."

If Mrs. Maiden heard the outburst, and I believe she did, she did not turn back, but busied herself in the tack room preparing for John the Farrier and Doctor Russ.

Claire did not require adult intervention. She responded to Trevor with equal venom in her voice. "Why do you even come out here? Why don't you just go back to wherever you came from? Go play baseball or something. Geez."

Claire turned her back to Trevor and began grooming me—a little more forcefully than usual, I might add.

Directed at any other student, I would have appreciated Claire's zealous defense on my behalf. But Trevor was different; slowly, we were working toward an understanding of each other. Undoubtedly, Mrs. Maiden and the boy's mother could detect no change in his demeanor, as he did stand in the corner every week for one solid hour. I could tell he was softening to me; he was opening just enough. He kicked out less and less each time. He had begun to sneak glances at me. He was behaving much like a horse. He needed to be left alone for long enough that his curiosity would overcome his anger or fear. We were making progress; I worried that Claire's harsh words might close Trevor to me for good, before I had come to know him at all.

The boy, at least, was interested enough to fight with Claire. He had held so much inside for so long, I suppose, that I should not have been surprised that Claire had opened up a rather clogged pipeline of emotions.

Trevor said nothing after Claire's outburst. He kicked the wall hard. Then he kicked it again. Down the line, the other horses danced around and gave half-hearted whinnies of displeasure. Across the way, Dante began kicking his own wall.

Claire brushed me roughly then turned to face Trevor. "And Chancey's not stupid! You're stupid!" She turned her back on Trevor.

All of the other horses turned to watch my room. Mrs. Maiden did not emerge from the tack room, nor did Mrs. Strickler. Stu, who had been mucking stalls, parked the wheelbarrow outside of Gwen's room, next to mine. He listened and watched but did not intervene.

Trevor did not hold back. He screamed at Claire, "My mom makes me come to this stupid place! I hate it here, and I hate your horse!"

Claire spun around to face him, but Trevor didn't let up. Trevor's lips sprayed saliva on my muzzle as he spoke. "It's an old, stupid, smelly horse. I wish it were dead!"

For the first time, Trevor stood right next to me. I could not see him, but felt and smelled that he was at my left cheek. He smelled precisely of an oatmeal cookie. In fact, I was certain a cookie, or part of a cookie, remained in his shirt pocket. Claire moved closer to my face and closer to Trevor. I had no trouble hearing either of them.

"Shut up! Shut up and leave Chancey alone, or you're going to wish you were dead!"

I nickered at Claire, trying to calm her down. I feared she had gone too far, but it was too late. The boy had egged her on purposefully, it seemed. In fact, I sensed that he needed someone, like Claire, to give him room and reason to say what came next, for he said it without anger, without any emotion, really.

"I am going to be dead. I have cancer and I am going to be dead. Don't say you're sorry, either. Don't say anything."

Claire did not speak, at first. She picked up a curry-comb and began circling it on the dirtiest part of my body, starting at my neck. Trevor remained in the room with us, and he did not turn back to the wall. He stood facing Claire, waiting for something. Finally, Claire spoke to him.

"Don't just stand there; pick up a brush. If you're going to come every week, you might as well have fun."

Trevor didn't budge.

Claire kept talking to him anyway. "When I first met Chancey, my parents were getting a divorce. I hardly remember anything about that time it hurt so bad every day. Everybody at school and at home started treating me differently, like they felt sorry for me or something. Even though I felt like a different person, I wanted to be the same person, and I wanted everybody to treat me like the same person. Does that make sense?"

Claire did not wait for Trevor to respond; Trevor remained silent. Claire had rarely spoken of her parents' divorce, though I knew her heart ached because of it. Claire continued talking to the stone wall of Trevor.

"What I do remember is that Chancey was always there for me. If I needed to talk, or be goofy and ride him backward, or just stand in his stall and smell him, it didn't matter. I was always his Claire, the same Claire every day."

She turned to look at Trevor, still silent. Claire kept talking to the air. "I know a divorce is not the same as cancer. For me, though, it's the hardest thing ever in my life. I miss my dad a lot when I'm with Mother. When I'm with Dad, I want to be with her. I know it's not the same, but it still hurts."

Trevor's posture softened. He put a hand on my cheek. Claire rested her head against me, perhaps remembering the day we met.

"Mrs. Maiden told me one time, 'Claire, you need to let your pain out and let love come back.' All I'm saying, Trevor, is the same thing. Chancey is good at letting love in. He will love you as deep as an atom is small, if you let him."

Claire put her arms around me and held me close. Then she turned and looked at Trevor. "Besides, Chancey has cancer, too. Y'all have something in common." Then Claire ignored him.

She had learned, from fraternizing with horses for so much of her childhood, that if you ignore us, our curiosity will almost always demand that you not. Neither Claire nor I were surprised when Trevor picked up the body brush and began brushing my neck alongside Claire.

"Slow down," corrected Claire. "Here, brush him like this, softer, in long strokes. See how he closes his eyes? That means he likes it." I closed my eyes again to demonstrate for Trevor.

Finally, Trevor spoke. "Does it really have cancer?"

Claire put the currycomb in the brush box and turned to Trevor.

"His name is Chancey. Here, I'll show you."

Claire moved around to my right side and pulled the lid of my eye down toward her hand. I stood still so that Trevor could see my cancer.

"See that kind of white-pink blob right there? That's

cancer. He has it in his left eye, too, but you can't see it because we had the tumor taken off that eye last month. But the cancer's still growing. He'll need another operation at some point. He's probably had six operations since I got him three years ago."

Claire released my eyelid and kissed me on the nose.

"Can it see?" Trevor asked about me.

Claire patiently repeated, "His name is Chancey." She waited for Trevor to repeat the question satisfactorily.

"Yeah, whatever. Can it see?"

"No, not 'yeah, whatever.' Chancey is his name; don't call him 'it.' To answer your question, *he* can't see on his left side, but *he* seems to see all right on his right. We did have to take a tumor off of his right eye last year, and this one will probably come off soon."

I had not let on to Claire that my right eye's vision had begun its deterioration. Mac and Gwen knew, and they covered for me quite well by always staying nearby and giving me guidance whenever I got into trouble in the field, mostly at night.

"Can you teach me to ride him?" Trevor asked. "Can you teach me to ride Chancey?" He repeated the question again with my name, to show Claire his sincerity.

"Sure! I'm an awesome rider and Chancey's an awesome horse. I'll teach you to ride, no problem. You'll be winning ribbons before you know it," Claire boasted.

The smells of sugar, oatmeal, and raisins right under my nose had caused me too much agony already. I nudged Trevor's shirt pocket very gently, certain that the remnants of an oatmeal cookie with raisins waited inside and hopeful that it waited for me.

Claire cocked her head. "What, Chancey?" she asked me, tickling my chin. Then Claire laughed. "Trevor, did you bring Chancey a treat?"

Trevor reached inside his pocket and pulled out half a cookie. "Oh, yeah. I don't like oatmeal cookies. So, I, uh, well . . ."

"You did! You brought Chancey a treat! You were going to make friends with Chancey on your own, weren't you?"

Trevor pushed his bangs around and stood looking at me. He made no move for the pocket that contained the cookie. I nibbled at his shirt. He laughed and reached inside.

"No, not like that," Claire ordered him. "Hold your hand out flat."

"You're so bossy," Trevor told her. "Are you always this bossy?"

He did as Claire told him, held his hand flat, and fed me the oatmeal cookie. I rested my head on his shoulder. He exhaled and began to breathe evenly.

The boy grew quiet. "Claire, I might not be able to get good enough to win a ribbon. That takes time."

Claire understood, as I did. Trevor meant he didn't have the time it would take to become an accomplished rider. Claire, being Claire, had no problem making big promises.

"Trevor, it won't take long at all. We'll have to pick the right event and you'll have to practice, but sure, no problem."

"Really? Like you think we could be champions?"

"Definitely, you two could be champions. But you have to promise two things. One, that you won't call Chancey stupid ever again, and two, that you'll try to have fun." Claire stuck her hand out to Trevor. Trevor accepted the deal and we set to work that afternoon.

# CHAPTER TWENTY-ONE

## *Under Claire's Instruction*

Over the summer Claire began working closely with Mrs. Maiden to teach Trevor to ride, forgoing her own time with me to focus on instructing Trevor. Despite his illness, Trevor was still a strong boy. Like Claire, he asked to learn everything right away. While Claire was content to just be near horses, whether mucking our rooms or feeding hay, Trevor was impatient to learn to ride and to win a blue ribbon. Having never won a blue ribbon, I had just about given up that goal for myself.

Claire never let Trevor cut corners. Whenever Claire would make Trevor go back to the barn to stretch me before riding, he would get frustrated. Trevor's impatience would show.

"Claire! We only have one hour; can't I just ride?"

"Okay, if you just want to argue with me for the fun of arguing, we can argue the whole hour. Or you can start stretching him right now and be done with it," Claire would insist.

She always won, and soon enough, Trevor did not forget to stretch me. Though I understood the boy's urgent need to learn quickly, I very much appreciated Claire's insisting that he care for me properly.

The first time he was in the saddle, Trevor kicked me hard in both ribs and shouted, "Yah, boy, yah!"

I did not move. I blinked my eyes twice to show Claire that I understood Trevor's request but would not respond.

"'Yah, boy'?" Claire laughed so hard her face turned dark. "Where'd you learn 'yah, boy'?" She tried to catch her breath.

Trevor giggled and squirmed around. "I've just always wanted to say it, that's all."

Trevor was motivated and fast to pick up the technical aspects of where to place hands and legs. For the first few weeks, Claire worked with him from the ground, teaching him to find his seat, making sure he placed his legs just behind the girth. He quickly grasped the idea of rising to the trot in time with my outside foreleg. He had more difficulty learning to ride with an open heart, but Claire was insistent that he must learn this, as well as how to post on the correct diagonal.

"Trevor, you're straight as a board. Relax. And don't forget to breathe. You're holding your breath," she scolded him. He did not immediately experience the contradiction of riding with a posture both straight and relaxed.

"You said, 'Sit up straight and tall.' I am sitting up straight and tall," he complained.

"Try this, Trevor. Sing your favorite song while you're riding. That will help you relax, and plus, you can't hold your breath while you sing."

"I don't have a favorite song," he protested.

"Seriously? You don't have a favorite song?" Claire was incredulous. "Do you know any songs?"

"My mom always sings a stupid one to me." He resisted Claire's suggestion.

Claire did not cut Trevor any slack, ever. "Everything can't be stupid all the time, Trevor. Okay, sing your mom's stupid song, even if you hate it. Sing it while you ride. Go ahead, sing."

Trevor asked for the trot and held his breath.

"Sing!" Claire screamed at him. She threw her arms in the air.

"All right, Claire. You can't get me to relax by yelling at me."

Claire laughed at Trevor because she knew he was right. "If you would just do what I say, I wouldn't have to yell."

That made Trevor laugh, and he began to sing his mother's song. *"'Tis the gift to be simple; 'tis the gift to be free.'"*

Right away, I felt Trevor relax. He loosened his hands, which had been tightly gripped on the reins; his back softened. Trevor began to breathe.

He sang on. *"'Tis the gift to come down where you ought to be. And when we find ourselves in the place just right, 'twill be in the valley of love and delight.'"*

People are often astonished at the nearly imperceptible movements and shifts that are felt by horses of their riders. I can feel where my students' eyes are looking. The slightest fidget of a seat feels like a tremor to me. I felt Trevor smile. We remained at a posting trot many times around the ring. Claire called out our instructions: "Now, add circles in your corners, but keep singing and keep posting."

Trevor's shoulders opened up, and he sunk deeper. What had been a tentative effort turned into a full serenade. *"'When true simplicity is gained, to bow and to bend we shan't be ashamed. To turn, turn will be our delight, 'til by turning, turning we come 'round right.'"*

"Now you've got it, Trevor. That's perfect," Claire praised him. She called for him to halt, which he did smoothly and gracefully. I squared my legs, so that Claire would compliment Trevor again.

"Look at you, Trev," Claire said. "Who taught you to halt Chancey square like that? I think you're ready to go on the trail. Hop down for a sec."

Trevor lowered himself to the ground tentatively and patted me on the neck. "Good boy, Chancey. You're making me look good to Claire."

One afternoon toward the end of August, after Trevor had been riding but three weeks, Claire unbuckled my saddle and hung it over the fence. She cupped her hands tightly together and gave Trevor a leg up.

Without a saddle, his rhythm improved and Trevor was able to mold his body to mine more easily. As Trevor felt the warmth of my own body, he relaxed the tension in his legs and core. He held my mane tightly with both hands, while Claire led us away from the ring and down to the river for Trevor's first trail ride. Though Trevor did exactly as Claire asked him to do, I could sense his uneasiness; Claire could, too.

"Relax, Trevor," Claire encouraged him. "Close your eyes and grab mane. Let Chancey carry you all the way down to the river. Don't be scared, okay?"

"Chancey," whispered Trevor. He held my mane in his hands and leaned forward to my neck. "I've got you, Chancey. I'm not going to let go, either."

We walked through a field of brand-new saplings of

every hardwood of the mountains, all fighting for their share of sunlight. I looked up and could tell by the bend in the canopy which direction the river flowed. Even if I could not have seen it, I would have known by the cool, damp change in the air how to get to the Maury River. I found that if I listened beyond the wind and the song-birds, I could hear the Maury River long before I could see it. Claire heard it, too. We halted.

"Listen," she told Trevor. "What do you hear?"

Trevor stretched out on my back; he took his time answering her. "I hear a woodpecker drilling that dead tree right there."

"What else?" Claire wanted him to name the river.

"I hear those annoying geese honking at each other," he answered.

"Hmmm. I hear them, too. What else?" she asked again.

This time Trevor heard the river. "Water. It sounds like cars driving by, but softer. That's the river."

Trevor sat up and again grabbed a handful of my mane, this time with only one hand. He shifted around excitedly.

"Look," Trevor shouted, "a belted kingfisher! My favorite bird! I like that spiky hairdo."

I turned my head far to the left to give my face full exposure to the right bank of the river. The kingfisher sat perched on a sycamore limb, searching for trout, a sure sign that the river was running clear.

Claire tied the loose end of the lead rope to my halter. "Scoot back," she bossed Trevor. "I'm hopping up there with you. I like being up high when I come up to the river."

Trevor slid back all the way to my tail to give Claire enough room. She grabbed my mane and hoisted herself up. Trevor moved forward and held Claire's waist.

"Will you sing that song for us the rest of the way?" Claire pleaded with Trevor.

"Claire, stop making me sing. I just want to sit here on Chancey."

"But your song is the most beautiful song I've ever heard and besides, Chancey likes it."

Trevor laughed at Claire, and began his song anyway. Just as the undergrowth of saplings gave way to tall, thick grass, the Maury River appeared. Claire let me stop and graze while Trevor finished his song. The wind from the river kept most of the flies away from me. The shade from the birch, leaning out far beyond the bank, protected my eyes from the sun.

"Have you ever been swimming with a horse?" Claire asked Trevor.

"You're such a show-off, Claire. You know I've

never been swimming with a horse. You've been with me every time I've ever been on a horse," Trevor teased.

"Okay, I was just asking," Claire said, pretending to be hurt. She thought for a moment, then rephrased her question to him. "Trev, what I meant was, do you want to go swimming with Chancey and me, right now?"

"Sure," Trevor answered. "If you think it's safe."

"Geez, Trevor. Stop being such a fraidycat. Hold on."

Both children slipped off their socks and shoes. Claire squeezed her legs and gave me a little kick. Claire clucked to encourage me, but it was an entirely unnecessary aid. I, too, wanted to swim. I walked slowly into the water, allowing plenty of time for my legs, and the children's, to adjust. Claire and Trevor both sucked in their breath the moment the river slapped their legs. I waded slowly out to my neck; Claire stood on my back and dove into the river. Trevor did not need coaxing from Claire to do the same.

The river was slow and seemed ready to fall asleep as we three splashed the afternoon away. We stayed in the water together until the breeze blowing off it became too cold for Claire. She started to shiver, and not liking to be cold, tied my lead rope back into reins. I carried the two of them back to the barn. For what was left of the summer, this became our habit. Trevor would arrive for his lesson with Claire, and we would end our time together with a trail ride to the Maury River.

Once summer turned to fall, Trevor was ready for a greater challenge—taking me on the trail without Claire at the head. Claire would accompany us on Mac; her goal was to simulate the conditions of the hunter pace that would occur at the Ridgemore Hunt in Rockbridge County at the end of November. Though I had hoped I would be paired with Claire for the Ridgemore Hunt, I considered it an honor and a privilege to carry Trevor.

# CHAPTER TWENTY-TWO

## The Ridgemore Hunt

At the start of the Ridgemore Hunter Pace, Mrs. Maiden tied our team pinny, number sixteen, around Claire's waist. Trevor and Claire looked very much the team, both turned out in what appeared to me to be matching jodhpurs, and both sporting brand-new Maury River Stables team jerseys, given to them by Mrs. Maiden. I swelled with pride; I could imagine no better teammates than Claire, Trevor, and Mac.

Practically the entire barn family, it seemed, had turned out to cheer us on. Mother, Stu, and Mrs. Strickler were all there to help out. Even my canine friend Tommy had joined us. As I had come to expect, Mother reached to my neck and gave me a pat; she did the same with Mac and Claire. "Be safe; have fun!" she said. Mrs. Strickler seemed nervous. She smoothed Trevor's shirt, brushed his bangs out of his eyes, and fidgeted with my bridle until Trevor made her stop it.

Our team was barely out of the start box when we came upon trouble with some young horses. Some of them refused to cross the brook at the start of the course. Horses and riders were backed up twenty deep; the situation was tense not only because of the green horses but also the green riders. Trevor wisely asked me to move around the trouble. I thought it quite brave of him, really, and was proud of the way he tried to overcome his own fear, which of course I felt because he stopped breathing.

Trevor held his breath, tightened his legs, and instructed, "Walk on, Chancey," with such resolve, that even if I had not already been intending to move away from the catastrophic backup at the start, I would have walked on anyway at the urgency and intent of his request. He glanced back at Claire and Mac and urged them to come with us. We both felt Claire move out, and so proceeded up the hill, leaving the green horses and their people to fret over a bit of cold mountain water running across the course.

The moment we reached the top, Trevor and I both realized that in our haste to break away from the others, we had allowed Claire and Mac to get cut off by a loud, domineering woman trying to organize the field of novices. I called down to Mac, "Come on! Don't waste any more time. You've placed Claire in harm's way. Walk on!"

Mac called quickly back to me, "The girl on the bay's the problem. She's having trouble."

I could see for myself that the situation at the brook had deteriorated. I was glad to be at the top of the hill, looking down, though I desperately wanted Claire and Mac beside us. The girl and her young bay causing the trouble were so worked up that panic was spreading like a wildfire through all of the horses. Green horses, especially green fancy horses, are rather unpredictable. Green girls, especially fancy girls, are rarely prepared to lead such horses, as was the case at the brook.

Mac and Claire, I could see, remained calm. I could hear Claire pleading with the hunt mistress to let them cross. Mac called to me regularly, letting me know the status of their progress up the hill. All of the horses below were dancing wildly, except for Mac, who stood, observing and, I could see, thinking of how to get around the situation, which was becoming more dangerous by the minute.

When the bay not only refused to walk on, but reared

up on her hind legs, the girl dismounted—a wiser decision than I had credited the young lady with the capacity of making. I hoped the young rider might lead her green mare across the stream and get back in the saddle once the mare understood that the water would not harm her. I was sure the incident would now be resolved.

My judgment was premature. Once on the ground, the girl took hold of her stirrup iron with a grip of such force that I had only seen prior in our John the Farrier at home when removing old shoes. She struck her horse, no doubt thinking that this beating might persuade the mare to eagerly cross the brook and win the race. The mare cowered, and from the top of the hill I could see her fear growing, for her ears were now pinned flat back, and from way atop the hill, the white of the mare's eyes was unmistakably visible even to me.

When the iron struck the mare the second time, I vehemently objected to the brutality. I neighed shrilly as if my doing so would sway the girl to stop. When the girl struck the mare a third and then a fourth time, I lost my composure and reared up, both in anger and in alarm, issuing a call to end the cruelty and also, again, urging Mac to get Claire safely up the hill. The green girl had just injected the mare with a lifetime fear of water. The mare would now associate crossing water with pain and a beating.

Yet again, the girl hit her horse with the stirrup iron,

only more forcefully did she strike. I reared once more. It was at the top of my second rear that Trevor, so patient until then, made his own fear known to me. He leaned his weight full into my withers, forcing all four of my hooves to the ground. It was the right thing for him to do, for it pushed me back to earth. Trevor was scared, and without Claire, forced to make all decisions by himself.

Trevor pleaded quietly in my ear, "Please, Chancey. Remember, I'm not Claire. I'm afraid now, so I'm getting off of you until you stop it. You're behaving too recklessly!" With that assertion, Trevor jumped out of the saddle and began leading me around, turning me away from the harsh scene below.

I felt ashamed, if truth be told, that I had frightened Trevor. And I felt relieved that he had turned me away from the beating so that I did not have to watch any longer. Trevor talked to me as he led me around the hill, telling me that Claire and Mac would join us shortly. He commented on the clear day and warm late-autumn air. It did feel almost like summer. My coat was already thick in preparation for winter to come. The air felt good while we were standing still at the top of the hill, though I knew that by the end of the race, Trevor and I both would be lathered and breathing fast. Trevor was already breathing too fast, but at least he was breathing. He started singing to slow down his breathing and gather back his courage. Claire had taught him well.

Trevor and I were relieved when Claire and Mac reached us. Trevor wasted no time—again I thought him quite brave—in jumping onto my back by using his own strength and determination. I rumbled at Mac and looked Claire over; both seemed well and ready to go.

Claire's strategy, as explained to us prior to the event, was first and foremost to get out of the start quickly and stay well away from the other teams. She aimed to keep our riding conditions as much like a trail ride as possible to minimize distractions for Trevor. Originally, she had planned to keep us trotting for much of the course, except at the hills, which we would canter up. Because of the early mishap, Claire now said we would need a much faster ride than any of us had planned.

She changed our strategy and relayed to Trevor and me, "If we're going to have a shot at this, Trevor, you've got to canter a lot more than you ever have done. Don't be scared; just trust Chancey and let him go. Chancey will stay with Mac and me. You stay with Chancey. Can you do that?"

I could feel Trevor's hands, already wet with perspiration, shaking on the reins. "I think so." I nickered at him to tell him I would not let him down, or off.

"Okay." Claire looked at Trevor directly. "Are you ready then?"

Trevor stalled. "No. I don't think I can do it, Claire. Forget it. This was a stupid idea."

Claire and Mac looked as though we had all the time in the world and this was just another day of trail riding in the mountains. Claire tried to convey her surety to Trevor. She backed Mac up until they stood right next to us.

"Shhh. Don't say that, Trev. We're a team, all four of us. Who cares if we win or not? We're going to finish together, and you can do it."

Trevor nodded.

Claire smiled at him and asked, "If you feel off at the canter, what are you going to do?"

"Uh, grab mane?" He sounded so unsure.

"Yes! Grab mane. Chancey won't let you down. Now, let's go—we have a hunter pace to win!" Claire and Mac cantered away. Trevor moved his right leg behind my girth; he did not have to ask for the canter, for I was determined to stay with Claire and Mac. Halfway across the field, Claire turned back and shouted, "Are you okay?"

Trevor could not speak, for he was not breathing. He did manage to nod. I did not break our canter until Claire and Mac slowed to a trot. Claire waited for us to pull alongside her. She was such a good leader, letting us know of every twist and turn and challenge in the course and how we could best take it as a team.

"We're going over the Maury next, but it's shallow and narrow. Breathe, Trevor, and chill. Chancey loves water; just stay with us. I want to get us out of this big group and by ourselves again."

Trevor again nodded. His head darted around, looking left, then right, at every other team near us. As his head turned, so did his shoulders, his hands, and his hips. It was difficult for me to keep from dancing around, for with each nervous movement the boy made, the bit in my mouth followed likewise. I could tell that being close to so many other horses had unnerved him. I knew, however, that his excitability was not to be mistaken for intentional communication with me. I followed Claire's instruction on the course. Once Trevor refocused, though his hands gripped the reins tightly, he posted expertly in good time with me.

When the course entered the forest for the first time, I felt sure that we must be nearing the halfway point. Up until then, the entire route had been up and down through open fields, much like our trails at home. As we entered the forest, we realized that the terrain had been deceitfully comfortable. None of us had anticipated a steep and slippery cliff down so far into a ravine that the bottom could not be seen.

Our competitors, evidently, had not anticipated this obstacle either. The forest floor was muddy from several days prior of rain. Only a few strides into the woods, the forest floor dropped off so steeply that I could not see below to the point where it would level off again. A gray pony in front of us lost her footing in the mud and fell to her knees before stabilizing and bolting through the trees, off course. When the pony bolted, she caused a cedar branch, rife with berries, to snap back into Claire's face. Claire did not lose her seat or her courage.

Claire may well have been afraid, but she did not choose fear as her advisor. She called back to Trevor, "Chancey's an App; he's made for this stuff. Do what I do: breathe and lean back. Lean way back. We're going down one step at a time."

Trevor breathed in deeply. He gave me my head and leaned back, keeping his center of gravity weighted exactly with mine. Had he been too far forward, no doubt, I would have slid easily. There was a point in our descent where both Claire and Trevor were stretched out flat on their backs, loosely holding on to Mac and me, allowing us to do the work. Neither child panicked once. I was proud of them both, especially Trevor.

Some horses behind us whinnied and bolted back up the cliff. I heard a rider thud to the ground. Trevor began to sing; he was breathing. Mac and I did not speak, but head to tail, we got down the cliff together. My Appaloosa feet served my team well. There was no hint of slipping or sliding, only an easy, steady walk in the forest. Trevor did his job of staying relaxed; I did my job of keeping Trevor safe.

When we reached the bottom, Claire turned back to us. "Awesome! Y'all are awesome!"

For the first time on the course, I felt Trevor relax. "We did it, Claire!" He patted me on the shoulder. "Chancey, we did it!"

Claire brought us back into the open field. "Don't get too fired up just yet. As soon as we're totally out of the forest, we've got to canter up that hill. Then we'll need to stop at the checkpoint and get our halfway chip. It doesn't count as a finish unless we turn in the chip at the end. Come on, let's go!" Claire and Mac cantered away, and I stayed right with them.

Finding the spot in the saddle that is secure and balanced is not easy. Claire is the only one I've known to find that spot right away, without effort and without fail. It's a spot where I feel the legs of my rider secure against me, almost holding us both up, moving us both forward together and in good time. If my rider can find the spot and hold it, we can achieve a unison that is not dependent on my eyesight. We can move together, galloping up hills, through forests, and over streams as if we are welded. Claire knows this spot on me, and I suspect on Mac and every other horse she has ever joined.

Trevor was a different story. He was, at times, consumed so greatly with his own fear that he failed to realize even the most obvious mistakes, such as placing the bridle on me upside down, in a convoluted mess. Often he sat high, perched up in the saddle, with all his weight gathered atop of me in a compact triangle on the saddle. Carrying Trevor sometimes felt as I imagined it would feel to carry two or three hay bales all stacked up on the saddle, and I was constantly shifting my own weight to keep the unstable tower from toppling over.

The hunter pace was the occasion that presented a perfect teaching moment to show Trevor how it felt to ride together, moving as a team. On one of the final hills, we cantered at first, and as I moved into a gallop, Trevor's imbalance caused him to grab my mane to keep from falling. Thankfully, he did not lean his weight onto my neck, nor did he pull back on the reins. He grabbed a handful of my mane to steady himself, and, as I had by now several times witnessed his courage, I was not surprised that though feeling unbalanced, he did not ask me to stop.

What I did next was risky to be sure, but I felt for the first time that Trevor was feeling confident. He was breathing. I could not see it, but I believe he was smiling. On this day, Trevor was riding with heart.

What I did, actually, was to lob him into the perfect spot. If I could have used words, I might have told him to sit deeply, close his knees around me, and drop his pelvis into me. I did not have words available to me, and, truthfully, Trevor had heard these words from Mrs. Maiden and Claire many times in his own lessons. He needed to feel what the words meant. I wagered that if I got Trevor into the spot on my own, he would feel it and know it was right. It happened just like that.

Midway up the hill at a gallop, I pushed Trevor into the right place. He stuck to me; he let go of my mane.

Trevor hollered through the wind to me, "Woohoo! We're flying, Chancey!"

He stayed in the right place throughout the remainder of the course, only once losing his left stirrup and even then not losing the spot. When I felt the loose stirrup slapping my barrel, I slowed enough for Trevor to pick it back up. As he did, he yelled to me, "Good boy, Chancey. Go on—I've got it!"

Trevor was one of two boys his age that I had observed on the field that day. The other boy and his paint pony each carried a girth that far exceeded that of anyone on our team, save Mac. As we neared the checkpoint, the chunky pony and her boy cut us off, inserting themselves directly behind Claire and Mac. Claire and Mac stretched out beyond us, not realizing that Trevor and I had been left behind. The pony and her boy challenged us to race them up the hill at a gallop.

Trevor, with his newly found confidence, leaned into

me and whispered, "Yah, boy! Yah!" I understood his command, and this time I welcomed it. Though already at a gallop, and nearing the end of my capacity, I reached down into my reserves to give Trevor the extra bit of speed that a command such as "Yah, boy" deserved. *This,* I thought, *is the greatest contest of my life.*

We galloped away from our challengers and caught Claire and Mac, who were waiting for us at the checkpoint. Claire encouraged Trevor to take the chip, so that he could officially represent our team at the finish.

"Are you sure?" Trevor asked Claire.

Claire nodded. "Come on, we're almost there!"

Trevor yelled over to Claire, "That kid was trying to race me! Did you see him?"

"The boy on the fat pony?" Claire gobbled up the challenge. She collected Mac's reins and dug her heels into his side. "Ever race a paint before, Trev? Easy peasy. There's no way he'll catch us."

Trevor pressed his heels into me with conviction. He clucked at me and yelled into the wind, "Yah, boy!"

The rest of the course was open, flat field, with only a few small hills left. Claire and Trevor galloped to the end, and both children hollered wildly when we spotted the Maury River Stables delegation standing near the finish, waiting for us. Mrs. Strickler and Mother were jumping up and down, clapping their hands together and holding on to each other like old friends. Mrs.

Maiden threw her head back and laughed. Stu pumped his fist in the air to show his support. Tommy tore away from his leash and ran up to me, sniffing each of my legs for a replay of the course we had run. I whinnied my gratitude to them all. Mac echoed my sentiment then and together, we four crossed the finish line of the Ridgemore Hunt unharmed and grateful for a victorious ride through the blue mountains, for, ribbon or no ribbon, all of us had ridden the hunter pace course exactly as it was meant to be ridden: with confidence, patience, strategy, and endurance.

Our fine team was exhausted after the Ridgemore Hunt. For the entirety of the race, Claire and Mac led the way through seven miles of beautiful gallop hills. All four of us needed refreshment. Claire hitched Mac and me to the trailer; Trevor tied fresh hay nets nearby. Trevor and Claire ran off together, still giddy from our race. Tommy curled up in the shade underneath me and took a nap. I felt quite content that day. Claire and Trevor, I knew, would soon return.

I was proud of Trevor and his many displays of courage throughout the difficult course. He had trusted me, and I had trusted him. I knew the boy was tired and was glad that Claire had taken him off to find food and water. I finished off the last of the hay in my net and remembered to thank Mac for taking such good care of Claire. He rumbled, but did not stop eating.

"We were a good team this morning, Macadoo. We should do this more often," I said, ignoring my quivering haunches. I tried to catch my breath. Mac was tied to the right of me, and though he was on my good side, I could hardly make him out. I attributed my clouded vision to the perspiration still running into my eye, as it had from our first canter up a hill. Mac must have sensed my difficulty, for he did not reciprocate the congratulatory praise. He inquired, with concern in his voice, "How are you, Old App?"

I had no opportunity to reply or form a response, for the children came sprinting back, bursting with some news.

Trevor and Claire each clutched a blue ribbon in one hand. The boy threw his arms around me. "Chancey! We won! We won the hunter pace!" Claire was laughing; she came to me first.

"I knew you could do it, pony. You're the best friend in the world. I knew you could do it! You made Trevor a champion!"

Then she whispered in my ear, "Next time, I'll ride you myself, like we planned."

She kissed me, then congratulated Mac and tucked her ribbon into his halter.

Trevor, likewise, tucked his blue ribbon into my halter and, more to show off his win than anything else, I'm sure, he untied me and we walked to the watering place. Seeing no one else around but some mares from the course, Trevor shared his grand news with them. "We won! Chancey, Claire, Mac, and I won! I've never won anything; I won today!" I rumbled low and affirmed my own elation. That day to one boy, I became a champion.

## ★ CHAPTER TWENTY-THREE ★
### Yah, Boy!

After the hunter pace, throughout the fall and into the winter, Trevor continued to come to the barn for his weekly riding lessons, but he did not ride. He resumed his earlier habit of standing in my room; this time I stood beside him. Trevor leaned his head out of the window, as is also my habit. I recognized that he was trying to catch the wind and nickered softly to him, letting him know he was welcome to remain as long as he liked, for Trevor was a champion; he had won us a blue ribbon. Claire often stayed in my room with him, and she never pressed him to ride.

"Look how blue the sky is, Chancey, and not a cloud to be seen. Snow will be here soon; can you smell it?" Trevor asked me.

I looked at Trevor, turned out in fresh riding clothes that smelled of plastic, not hay or dirt. I understood then that our riding together as a team had come to an end.

I was content to stand with him, noting every change in the sky and clouds for many days in a row. He loved to describe for me every hawk and pileated wood-pecker he spotted. He explained to me that which I already knew—how the river birch, clustered just below the gelding field, told us in which direction we would find the Maury River.

Trevor also told me much that I did not know; I was happy to listen to all he had to say, and so was Claire. During these times, Claire spoke not a word, but would sit atop me or lean against me and listen to Trevor teach us about the natural world around us.

"Chancey, did you know that in some other moun-tains, far away in Utah, there lives a stand of forty-seven thousand aspen trees that are really all the same organ-ism? That's the largest living organism on Earth. Can you believe it? I've been there myself, and it's amazing to think that all of those trees grow from the same exact root system: all one tree. If you cut one down, it wouldn't die; another would grow in its place."

Trevor closed his eyes. I closed mine, too, in order to imagine such an aspen grove. He leaned into me and grew quiet. Then he whispered, "I wish I could see Utah again."

We never competed together again, but the three of us often walked down to the river together. Whatever the weather, we three enjoyed the trail to our private spot. Trevor usually sat on my back, while Claire was content to lead us both, as long as Trevor would promise to sing. Even though it was too cold for swimming, the two friends would hop across the rocks, Trevor always on the lookout for the belted kingfisher.

My eyes were failing me more than I had revealed to anyone. Even Claire did not realize the loss that I had endured. So strong was my trust in those around me— Claire, Mother, Stu, Mrs. Maiden, Tommy, Mac, Gwen, and even Daisy—that it was easy to hide the truth of the darkness that had taken over my right eye.

Before anyone else noticed, it was Mac who witnessed me walking into fences and gates. He never let on, but he did keep closer to me at those times of the day when we were either being turned out or brought into our rooms. When Mac was near, I could smell sunflowers on him. Like me, Mac received special supplements to his grain twice daily. Mine was to ease my pain; Mac's was to keep his coat shiny since he was showing nearly every weekend. Had I not been able to smell my friend, I would have felt the ground tremble whenever he came galloping up to me.

"This way, Old App. Come this way." He would guide me through the gate or toward fresh hay. We never discussed my worsening condition, but Mac surely knew first.

I found it fairly simple to continue my routine with almost no interruption. In my therapeutic work, the sidewalkers flanked me on both sides, guiding me around the ring and through simple courses. While Claire and Mother were still my sidewalkers, Mrs. Strickler had also become certified and occasionally replaced Claire in the ring. None of my therapeutic students were trotting or cantering, and I had long ago retired from jumping. In fact, the last jump I had attempted was at Tamworth Springs. No one had realized yet how rapidly my eyesight had declined, though none would have been surprised to learn of it, for we all had expected this day would come.

While Mac may have been the first to detect the true state of my eyes, Claire was the first to speak of it. Claire's discovery came on a day of sorrowful circumstances for us both. It was the afternoon that we received the news Trevor's cancer had returned full force.

One late winter afternoon, as we eagerly awaited the day when springtime finally returned to the blue mountains, Claire was in my room grooming me. She did not intend to ride, only to pamper me a bit. We had no show to prepare for; Claire was pulling my mane because she knew I would enjoy it. In fact, I had nearly dozed off when Trevor's mother appeared at my door, without Trevor.

"Hi, Mrs. Strickler," Claire said. "Where's Trevor today?"

Mrs. Strickler walked into my room and patted me on the neck. She did not answer Claire's question; instead she asked, "Claire, how are you?"

I felt Claire step back from Mrs. Strickler. I turned my head to Claire's voice. "Wh-what's that in your hand? Why do you have Trevor's blue ribbon?" Claire stopped breathing.

"Claire." Mrs. Strickler moved closer to me and steadied herself on my neck.

She started again. "Claire, Trevor wants Chancey to have this ribbon. I promised him I would bring it over today." Mrs. Strickler tucked the ribbon into my halter. She patted my neck again, then smoothed her hand over the ribbon. I recalled how she had smoothed Trevor's shirt in much the same way on the day we won.

Claire's hand breezed by my face; she snatched the ribbon out of my halter. "No! This is Trevor's ribbon; he won it. I have a blue ribbon from the Ridgemore Hunt at home, and T-Trevor, Trevor has one."

I felt Claire's hand shake beneath my mouth, as I stood between the two. "H-here, this is Trevor's." Again, she tried to make Mrs. Strickler take the ribbon back to her son. Mrs. Strickler was silent. I could feel the two of them looking at each other.

Mrs. Strickler sighed and softly placed the ribbon back in my halter. She touched the ribbon again, and ran her hand slowly from my neck to my withers. Then she addressed me, not Claire.

"Chancey, Trevor is going home soon. He wants you to have this ribbon. He hopes that you will remember how the two of you beat the boy on the fat pony. He especially asked me to give you a message."

Mrs. Strickler put her mouth to my ear and whispered, "Yah, boy, yah."

Then she turned back to Claire and took my girl's hands. Her voice barely made it out of her throat. "Thank you, Claire, for treating Trevor like Trevor. He asked me to give you this. . . ." Mrs. Strickler leaned across me and kissed Claire's face. Then she left my room.

I heard Claire turn away from the door and walk to the window in my room. I moved toward the sound of her breath and waited for her to call me nearer. I did not wait for long.

"Chancey?" Claire called. "Pony, we're not going to see Trevor again."

I took two steps and bumped into Claire. I blew a long breath out. Claire blew back into my nose.

"Come on, Chance. Let's go for a ride."

She did not tack me up with a bridle or saddle or even a bareback pad. Claire clipped a lead rope to my halter and escorted me out of the barn. She walked at an urgent pace past the mare field. Daisy and Princess cantered up alongside us, eager to know where we were going. I whinnied my uncertain reply. We passed my paddock, where Gwen and Mac were already turned out; they called out the same as the others.

Claire stopped at the gelding field; Dante threatened to block our entrance. Claire popped Dante's rear hard enough to make him whinny and canter away. I waited for Claire to guide me through the gate. She clucked at me to hurry up, but I could not see my way through. As she had done so many times in our friendship, Claire tied my lead rope into reins, grabbed hold of my mane, and pulled herself onto my back. When she was a little girl, she would wiggle and writhe to make it up without help. Now she pushed herself up with ease. She squeezed my barrel and called into my ear, "Yah, boy! Yah!" We cantered away.

For the length of the gelding field, Claire never allowed me to break stride. Her calves stayed firmly planted, and she leaned forward, asking for a gallop.

"Yah, boy!" she called again. The other geldings whinnied at us to stop. From our field, Mac called out to me, "The fence, Chancey! She's running you into the electric fence!"

I thought surely Claire could see the fence, for I could not. She began counting, "One, two, one, two." Claire intended to jump the electric fence. I readied myself, knowing there was nowhere for me to duck. I listened for my cue. My muscles remembered what it felt like to jump, and they began to twitch. "One, two, one, two, one, two, *jump!*"

Claire held me tight, rose into jump position, and lifted me up over the electric fence. She gave me my head, and though I could not see it, I felt that we had easily cleared the height. The geldings galloped right up to it and called out to us. We did not turn back. Claire galloped me through the river where we had swum so often with Trevor. She held her legs firm and stayed right with my center of gravity, encouraging me to scurry up the river's right bank. Claire was taking me to Saddle Mountain.

We cantered up the old logging trail, never stopping until we had almost reached the peak. Claire jumped down and untied the lead rope, allowing me to graze what grass and sarsaparilla I could find. I kept near Claire, and when I could no longer hear her breath, I rumbled out to her. "Up here, Chancey. I'm sitting up here." I walked on until the terrain became rockier and I smelled Claire directly at my feet. I dropped my head down to her, and she wrapped her hands around my neck.

Claire was shivering cold. I tossed my head up and down to indicate that we should head back; Claire did not budge. She sat, freezing on a boulder, and, I can only presume, looking down at the Maury River Stables below us. I positioned myself to guard Claire from the wind. I felt the shadow of storm clouds gather around us. The air had grown damp and thick; I could taste that we were standing in a cloud. Claire's teeth knocked against themselves violently. She would not leave.

I pushed my nose under Claire's arm; she rebuffed me. "Stop, Chancey." I pushed against her again.

"Stop it, I said. Stop."

Now Claire was turning away from me. I wondered what would have happened that day many years ago, when I first turned my back on Claire, if she had left my room as I had asked. She might never have come back. I might never have lived this life at the Maury River Stables. I tried to recall what she had told me that day. "Let love come back," Claire had said. "Let love come back to you."

I rested my head on Claire and gently nodded into

her shoulder. She paid no mind to me or the winter air. Appaloosa horses grow fine, thick coats; I was happy to share mine with Claire. I moved closer in to her so that I could protect my girl from the harsh wind blowing across Saddle Mountain. So deep were we in winter that the trees atop the mountain could not deter the winds from ripping into us. Claire had never liked the cold.

In the shelter of my withers, Claire grieved for Trevor. I grieved with her, though it would be false for me to claim that I did not also rejoice, for Mrs. Strickler had told me herself Trevor was going home.

Finally, Claire stopped shivering. She held me to her face and warmed her bare hands against my coat. "I love you, Chancey. Let's go back."

Claire dried her eyes on my neck, stood up, and tucked her body close into me, seeking warmth. Again, she pushed up onto my back. I waited for some direction from her, for I could not see. The mountain was pulling at me to go down, but I could not determine how steep the grade. Earlier in our friendship, I would have done all the work and carried Claire back to the barn without any need of direction whatsoever. Claire had steered me up Saddle Mountain; Claire would have to steer me down.

"Come on, boy, go on," Claire urged. Yet she did not pick up the makeshift reins. I did not move. I waited for guidance from Claire. She grew impatient with me, which I understood, for she had yet to realize that I needed her to be my eyes now.

"What's wrong, Chancey? Can't you see I'm ready to go?" I did not answer, and I did not move.

"Oh, no. Oh, no." Claire jumped off me, not on my left side as is customary, but on my right. She stood next to my face, I could feel her there.

"Oh, no." I felt her arm jerking back and forth.

"Can't you see my hand?" Claire cried. "Can't you see my hand?" I rumbled softly into Claire's ear. There on top of Saddle Mountain, Claire discovered that I was now blind. She did not panic. Claire grabbed my mane and jumped up again.

I felt her legs even and firm on my barrel and her steady application of evenness from both hands. She pushed gently with her seat.

"Walk on, pony. Walk on."

I stepped out, tracking straight until Claire invited me to turn right. Claire was riding as she always did and I trusted her, as I always had. She led me down the mountain, encouraging me every step. "I've got you, boy—don't worry." I was not worried; I was with Claire.

As I stepped into the Maury River on our return home, a light snow began falling on us. I heard no birdsong, nor did Claire sing for us—only the sound of my hooves splashing in the river interrupted the silence.

The mares and geldings all stood lined up along the fence watching for our return home. Stu was there, too, to disable the electric fence and allow us to walk over it. As Claire and I walked through the gelding field, each of my former fieldmates offered a word of welcome to me. Gwen and Mac rumbled affectionately, glad to have Claire and me safely back before the snow picked up. We made our way to the barn. There at the end of the line, in the mare field, stood Daisy, who announced for all to hear, "There goes a great horse."

## ✶ CHAPTER TWENTY-FOUR ✶
### *Fulfillment*

Have, then, Dam's prayers for me been answered? When I pass through every memory, as far back as I am able, I arrive at only one answer to this question. My life itself has been a long, prayerful response to my Dam and the fire star. In thinking back to the first echo of my heart, I do not find Monique and her disappointment in me. Nor do I even find Dam and her protection. I find the blue mountains.

I was born here and am grateful that, though I was nearly forced once to leave, I shall remain here forever. Though I will never travel through all of them, I have traveled the mountains enough, along the Maury River and beyond, to know that what can be seen from my room is only their beginning. I am sure the blue mountains go on and on. It comforts me to know that whether I can see them or not, I will always be surrounded by the mountains and the river.

These mountains have watched me grow blind. Yet in the time it has taken me to become an old and failing horse, the mountains have aged but a second. I cannot see, and I am not afraid. Standing here now, in my field with Gwen and Mac, some greater vision has replaced my eyesight.

Here, at the Maury River Stables, is where I will remain for as many more days as I am granted. More than once, I have heard Mother instruct Mrs. Maiden that I am to always occupy the corner room because of its ample space. I have no anxiety about my future and the care that I shall receive, nor do I need to search for food or water, as once I did. I fear nothing and am certain that of the many horses whose end will come in Lynchville, or some similar place, I shall never be among them.

Though I am now entirely blind, I do not lack a meaningful purpose, for I am surrounded by friends. I cannot see them, but I know when they are near. I continue my work with the therapeutic school; my students continue to pray for me every night, and I for them. My former student Kenzie comes often, too; she is helping me learn to be blind. Even Zack has been known to stop by for a visit.

Claire and Mother still agree that though Claire's talent has surpassed my own, we are family and will remain bound forever. Now that Claire is away, studying at a university at the edge of the blue mountains, Mother comes most often to hold me for the farrier or pull my mane. These days, sleep comes easiest to me when my mane is being pulled. I can smell when it's Mother coming up behind me. She always carries a stud biscuit in her pocket. Mother's skin smells cleaner than the sweat and grain that Mrs. Maiden wears on her skin. Even if I could not recognize Mother from the smell of her skin, I would know her by the way she sneaks around my face and reaches above my cheek to kiss me.

She speaks quietly to me. "Oh, I love this soft silky spot. That's my spot." She presses her lips deep into my head the same as she has always done.

Claire continues to visit me as her school schedule allows. When she comes home, she takes such an interest in grooming me herself that I confess there are times when I indulge in rolling deep into a briar patch without fear of being admonished. Claire still seems especially content to pull the briars out of my forelock, as she has done for so many years now. She is unfazed by my blindness. Where once she came to me, a small child with a big spirit who needed the mounting block to reach my mane, Claire now stands eye to eye with me.

Those days when Claire comes home fill me with joy! Claire still tacks me up in the same way she has done for what must be ten years now, for the new dentist recently observed that I am in my early thirties. In the ring, Claire guides me surely through my paces, keeping her calves tight on me, holding me up, and guiding me on. She likes to reassure me, "I've got you, Chancey. I've got you." Then, together, we pop over a tiny fence; it still feels as if we are each other's wings.

After warming up in the ring, Claire asks me, "Whaddya say, Chance? Are you up for a nice gallop through the mountains?" She does not wait for me to nicker, though I always do. Claire takes off the saddle and rides me bareback across the Maury River, up the right bank, and into the blue mountains. When I feel her ask for the canter with a light squeeze, I wait until Claire whispers two words before giving in.

"Yah, boy," she tells me softly. "Yah, boy!" she yells into the wind.

Though I can no longer see any of the trail before me, the eye of my heart sees perfectly well—just as clearly as if I had never been marked by this cancer. I can see Claire in her overalls, tenderly reaching the mask around my eyes to protect them from the sun. I can see the moment that changed me—forever.

Shortly after my arrival at the Maury River Stables, Claire had reached out to touch my marred face. I stood before her. I was malnourished, soiled, and nearly used up. I had wanted to save her from loving me and being disappointed. I know now that Claire loved me the very second that I loved her, and so she already knew everything about me that she needed to know. What she did not yet know she would come to accept with a greater compassion toward me than I ever thought possible, except, perhaps, from my own dam. Claire would not leave me to feel sorry for myself; Claire would continue to love me.

She never saw me as the castoff that I had become, abandoned in a field. Instead, she saw the horse that I was born to be, the great horse that the stars foretold on the night of my birth. Yet more than the stars could ever have predicted, I know that if I have been made great, at all, it is due entirely to the prayers of Dam and the love of Claire. So here I will stand, facing Saddle Mountain, listening for the whisper of Claire's return, and offering back all that I am now able, an infinite thanksgiving for this truly blessed life I have lived.

# ACKNOWLEDGMENTS

Thanks, Lance, for not shooting the albino buck in Cartersville. Thank you, Penny Ross, the Glenmore Hunt, Rhodes Farm at Wintergreen, the Stables at the Homestead, and Deb Sensabaugh of Virginia Mountain Outfitters for offering breathtaking hacks through the Blue Ridge and Allegheny Mountains. Thanks to Kathy, Judith, Elizabeth, and Rebecca for taking me on my first hunter pace and encouraging me to let Albert run. JEA, here's to our pretty fourth-place ribbon! Never has research been so invigorating! For teaching me about therapeutic riding: Kathy Pitt of Smooth Moves in Powhatan, Virginia, and Sue Alvis of Ride On in Glen Allen. Small programs like these, all over the country, perform miracles every day with incredibly dedicated volunteers and devoted horses.

Thank you to the brilliant horsewomen—Judith Amateau, Gail Bird Necklace, Kate Fletcher, Beth Lindsay, and Jennifer Wright, DVM—and brilliant readers—Leigh Amateau, Deanna Boehm, Cindy Ford, Mary Ellis Gregg, Mary Kiger, Maggie Menard, Betty Sanderson, and Amy Strite—who read, and improved on, an early manuscript. Thank you to Mrs. Ford, librarian, and the talented writers of the Guild of Youth Authors at Midlothian Middle School in Midlothian, Virginia. Thank you to the Irvine/Grue family of House Mountain Inn in Lexington, Virginia, for their hospitality and mountain retreat, perfect for imagining Chancey and Claire.

Thank you, my agent, Leigh Feldman, of Darhansoff, Verrill, & Feldman, who made me promise never to write "Neigh!" (Did I keep the promise? Yes!) Always, thank you to my Key West godparents: Judy, David, and Mark, for their gracious, generous time and friendship.

Candlewick Press rocks! I love all y'all: Brittany Duncan, Kate Fletcher, Sherry Fatla, Sharon Hancock, Anne Irza-Leggatt, Caroline Lawrence, Tracy Miracle, Chris Paul, Nicole Raymond, Jennifer Roberts, Charlie Schroder, Elise Supovitz, Ginny Wallace (hi, Ginny!), and most especially, Karen Lotz, collaborator extraordinaire. K—every second with you and this book has been exactly, perfectly wonderful. I had so much fun—thank you! (Also, very important: Karen, I just don't think I would have met *my boy* Ray had it not been for you. SI.)

I give major props to Bubba—my best friend, my true love—for supporting Judith's and my passion for all things equine. Back at you on all things bovine, baby!

Most of all thank you to King Albert, our albino Appaloosa witch, and my daughter, Judith, a truly gifted writer and creative partner. I love you.